CONSTANCE:

OR,

THE STAR OF THE BALLET.

———————

AN INTERESTING NARRATIVE.

————————

LONDON:

PUBLISHED BY G. PURKESS, COMPTON STREET, SOHO.

PREFACE.

ALTHOUGH the following tale records the events of years long past, yet the revelations presented in its pages, of the dangers that beset the career of the the "Star of the Ballet," may meet their parallel even at the present period. The history of the stage has afforded us too many instances, that the path of the female aspirant for histrionic fame is surrounded by temptations and difficulties which nothing but a strong mind and a virtuous education can enable her to surmount.

There are still antiquated debauchees, like Lord Headington, prowling about the side-scenes and the green-rooms, ready to lay the vilest plots for unsuspecting innocence ; there are still men of birth and education, whose reckless and extravagant habits render them the obsequious tools of wealth in the most scandalous actions. And, to turn to a brighter side of the picture, there are still generous souls, like Arthur Edmonstone, and other characters here represented, able and willing to aid virtue in distress.

The reader cannot fail of being interested in the adventures of Constance de Raincy, and will acknowledge that the good fortune which ultimately attends her efforts, was fully deserved by her courageous rejection of wealth and ease when accompanied by dishonour.

London, February, 1848.

CONSTANCE:
OR,
THE STAR OF THE BALLET.

THE BALLET AT THE PALACE—SEE PAGE 4.

CHAPTER I.

OUR heroine was born in London in the old-fashioned times of George the Second. Her father, by birth a Frenchman, after many years' service in a subordinate station, became partner in a mercantile firm of good standing. The wife of Monsieur, or—as he had been long resident in England, we should rather say —Mr. Le Raincy—fled, in her youth, from the south of France to escape the fate of the unfortunate Protestants so unwisely (as well as cruelly) persecuted by the fourteenth Louis. In London she married Mr. Le Raincy. Their only offspring

No. 1.

was our young heroine, Constance, now about ten years of age, who inherited from her mother a complexion clear, pale yet lustrous—eyes of the deepest jet—with a form shooting up in rivalry of the tall, slender figure of the maternal parent.

At the age mentioned, the health of Constance grew delicate, and by the advice of the physician, the merchant removed his family to Kensington—much, indeed, to the disadvantage of business-pursuits ; but he was amply rewarded by the improved looks, and livelier spirits of the invalid.

The family were fortunate in their neighbour, Mr. Edmonstone, a retired citizen ; fortunate, inasmuch as his son, Arthur, was but two years older than Constance, and soon became her favourite and playmate. As their respective gardens were separated only by an open fence, they had daily, hourly, opportunities of seeing each other; the little maiden (whenever the weather at all permitted) preferred the open air to indoors, which was especially pleasing to the Le Raincys, as it accorded with the regimen prescribed.

Conversing through the fence—far less obdurate obstruction than the stone-wall which separated the lovers of the olden time—exchanging the products of their gardens—narrating marvellous stories, and other childish pastimes, commenced an intimacy, which was strengthened and cemented by the permitted introduction of a ladder, enabling Arthur to achieve descent into Mr. Le Raincy's territory, and also to exhibit his gallantry in assisting Constance to alight within his own garden, in search of choicer raspberries, or to aid her in bringing to the ground, fruits of loftier growth.

Contrary to what might have been expected, this childish intimacy did not lead to any extended intercourse between the families. Mr. Edmonstone, a widower, was perhaps as much pleased as the Le Raincys, that his child was so innocently and pleasantly engaged, instead of seeking playmates at greater distance from home, and of course less known ; but whether from pride, reserve, or that each waited for the other's advances, or from causes operating unconsciously on both parties, a few neighbourly attentions were all the civilities that passed. They lived and moved in different circles, remained almost entirely ignorant of each other's connexions and affairs, and continued comparatively strangers, without any cause either of dislike or prejudice, or sense of offence to account for such estrangement. But it never entered the heads of Constance and her playmate to inquire why their parents were not more sociable. The young folk lived in a world of their own— the fairy-land of childhood ; their mode of intercourse and visiting possessed a touch of unconscious romance more congenial than the ordinary means of introduction, in company with parents or friends.

For two long years their happiness endured. Constance was educated at home ; Arthur's school was distant but a quarter of a mile. Intimacy was unlimited, unrestrained. In early morn they were seen together, and at close of a long summer's day, when Mrs. Le Raincy recalled her daughter within the house, lest her health should suffer from the evening air, they scarce bade each other adieu, conscious of a reunion on the morrow.

But all joys fade, all happy states of life cease, and live only as bright spots of memory. Le Raincy died suddenly, and it was discovered that the firm, of which he had been so long a partner, was not far removed from insolvency—at least it was so explained to the widow. Her own connexions in England dead—without assurance of a home, or even a place of refuge, in France, for her family had been dispersed and slaughtered by the dragoons of Louis—she had no other resource than to write an account of her impoverished condition to her late husband's brother, a resident of Paris. He was a thriving music-seller, to which trade was added the repair and sale of musical instruments, an occupation which brought him much in contact with various classes of professionals connected with the Parisian opera.

The widow was requested, or rather ordered—for the tone of the letter was harsh and unfeeling—to sell off effects and repair to Paris with the young Constance, Glad to escape from a neighbourhood, where she had lived in comparative affluence—of which in her changed state she was painfully reminded — the bereaved lady lost no time in quitting Kensington. The slight intimacy between the Le Raincys and Mr. Edmonstone required but formal leave-taking. A visit of ten minutes duration sufficed to announce her intention and exchange adieus, in course of which Mr. Edmonstone expressed regret at losin g an excellent neighbour, which was reciprocated by the lady observing that she was sorry to quit the spot, and that Constance would lose an amiable playmate.

And how parted the young people? Sorrowfully, yet full of hope. Life was so luxuriant in promise—the long vistas projected by the imagination were so rife of pleasant days to come,— no dark cloud hung over the future—that it was long ere they knew, and felt, the unhappiness of being severed. They would write often ! Arthur would save up money to visit France ! And he would now apply himself more ardently than ever to the study of the French language.

So parted Constance and her young friend.

In the music-seller the widow found a hard, selfish kinsman, disposed to avail himself to the utmost of her services, to requite the cost of maintenance. The education of Constance was yet very incomplete. As the time of Mrs. Le Raincy was fully occupied by household duties, and attendance on customers, she was very desirous that her daughter should be sent, for several years, to a seminary, the expence of which she offered to make up by extra labours and privations.

This plan was totally negative by Monsieur Le Raincy. He had other views, he said, more beneficial. Schooling she wanted, and should have, but it was the tuition of the professors of of the Academic Royale de Musique, (as the opera establishment in Paris was designated,) which would result far more advantageously than any other course of instruction. The figure and deportment of Constance, had he said, attracted the notice of the principal professor of the ballet. She would prove, he told Le Raincy, a valuable pupil, and doubtless become a *danseuse* of celebrity. It was rather an advanced age for the young demoiselle to commence, but she had advantages—beauty, slenderness of form, grace of movement—that it was throwing herself away if she adopted any other profession.

To this discourse the music-seller listened attentively. The ballet-master, he perceived, was an enthusiast; and a good bargain might be made—for himself. Of the present or ultimate advantage to Constance, he thought but little; and without consulting either mother or daughter, entered into an engagement with the professor, taking especial care that the emoluments accruing after several years preparatory tuition—which were to increase yearly till the term of engagement expired —should be receivable only by himself.

Mrs. Le Raincy was grieved beyond measure. She remonstrated, threatened, appealed, but in vain ; her brother-in-law was acting under the assumed responsibility of guardian of his niece, and as the mother had hitherto acquiesced in the assumption, it was now too late to dispute his authority—without funds, legal assistance, or friends to aid.

Constance, during initiation, lost much of the society of her mother. Her only consolation sprung from the kindness of the professor, who felt pure enthusiasm for an art, in the exhibition of which many people see only vices and depravity. In his vain, though sincere, estimation, it ranked far above statuary and painting, and he endeavoured to inspire, in his pupils, some portion of his own extravagant rapture. His life was irreproachable, his temper kind, and if the pupils could not elevate their views to his ideal standard, they were at least willing to devote themselves zealously to the accomplishment of his wishes, seeing that their diligence afforded him so much delight,

Constance was gifted with imagination, which her preceptor was not slow in discovering, and he encouraged her to study poetry and history—not for their own sake—but as affording hints for display of his beloved art. The exercise of mind which reading brought into play was beneficial, although not wholly in the direction contemplated by the ballet-director. It induced reflection, which gradually enlarged the mental vision beyond the duties of her profession, and the confined arena of the ballet. Oft contemplating remembrance of England with regret, her thoughts reverted to the lost, but unforgotten, home in Kensington—to the garden, the scene of so much innocent delight—to her playmate, Arthur. Should they ever meet again? Hope whispered—yes! but there was a dark cloud over the present which it was impossible to penetrate.

Meanwhile, as years flew on, Constance acquired a liking for her profession. In the interludes of the grand opera, performed before Louis and the court, ballets were introduced, the composition of her master, in which she bore a part, and was noticed as a pupil of exceeding promise. The beauty, which in childhood elicited admiration, now excited warmer feelings in the gay Parisian youth, awakening the fears and solicitude of Mrs. Le Rainey.

To consol the widowed parent, Constance drew flattering pictures of the future. The term of engagement expired, mistress of herself, she would rescue her mother from the servitude to which she was doomed by the griping music-seller! Resolution to achieve a parent's independence led to increased pains to arrive at excellence; efforts which were rewarded by the smiles of the director, by the applause of delighted audiences, and which were fondly attributed by the former, exclusively, to love of the profession. The melancholy which oft seized her spirits, which she could not always conceal, he surmised had other origin than grief or despondency, as both her present condition and future prospects were flattering and full of hope. With paternal solicitude he sought her confidence. Too ingenuous to deny sorrow, yet both ashamed and afraid to confess the tyranny of her uncle, and its effects on the health and spirits of her mother, she attributed her melancholy solely to regret at leaving England—never hearing from friends left behind; and then with a little artifice (to lend consistency to the explanation) she launched into a highly-coloured description of her happy life in the sea-girt land, concluding with a narration of the intimacy with Arthur, from whom she never heard. —a dear friend lost for ever!

The director shook his head, as though she had not told the whole truth. It was his impression, that spite of long absence, her feelings for her playmate had deepened with years, into an ardent passion which preyed on itself. However, nothing further passed, till he one evening carried her to the palace (a guest behind the scenes) to witness a ballet which he composed for the juvenile branches of the royal family, and in which several of the youthful scions of the Bourbon dynasty took part.

Constance, to her surprise, beheld the history of her own childhood. The incidents were identical, even to minute details. But for the tame scenery, and sombre costume of England, were substituted the mountains and glaciers of Switzerland—in lieu of suburban villas, picturesque cottages protected by an ascending forest of larch and pine, whilst the foreground was embellished with the gay dresses of the Swiss peasantry. The parting of the youthful lovers terminated the first act.

Constance, agitated and distressed, looked around to chide and scold her instructor, but he was not visible.

The curtain again rose. Years had elapsed, the old people were much older, The little damsel had shot into womanhood, an object of rivalry among rustic swains—but she rejects them all. A young *militaire*, with the epaulets of a captain, enters the stage. He very anxiously surveys both cottages—then the merry group assembled for the dance—starts on beholding the maiden, but recovering self-possession, conceals his features by drawing the cap closer over his brow. With an air of nonchalance he approaches the damsel, solicits her hand as partner for the dance, which—after a moment's pause—she yields. Tired with the gay amusement, he leads her to a seat, and whispering in her ear, she utters a cry of surprise, and flies toward the cottage-door. She is met by his aged father, who instantly recognizes the gallant. The hands of the young couple are joined, and the curtain descends amidst the applause of the illustrious and gratified audience.

The falling drop shut from the view of Constance the brilliant parterre crowded with rank and beauty. She stood alone, behind the scenes, in deep reverie, heedless of the busy supernumeraries, upon whom her eye—in vacancy—fell. Startled by a footstep, she turned and beheld—the professor. He led her, in silence, to the carriage, and as they rode homeward, inquired her opinion of the ballet.

She made no reply.

The first act he remarked, was her own ; he was not responsible for it. The second was, indeed, his conception, but it depended on herself whether he proved a true or false prophet.

"Monsieur has sadly abused my confidence," murmured Constance, "I perceive, in future, I must confine myself to the old father at the Carmelites."

"I might have made what I pleased of the second act," continued the ballet-director, without noticing her remark. "but as you will opine, I am disposed to look at the bright side of things."

A sudden glare of torch light, flashing through the carriage window, betrayed a tear glistening in her eye.

Taking her hand, he bade his pupil dispel every melancholy foreboding. Her destiny, he said, depended on herself—was very much in her own hands, even as the *denouement* of the t ifle which produced at the palace, was the choice of his will. Love of, combined with intense practice in, her profession would enable her to attain an eminence which must overcome the impediments of time and space—lay England at her feet, and all it contained, even the Arthur of her childhood. "And is not our art expressive ?" continued the enthusiast, " it searches every feeling ; lays bare the inmost recesses of the heart with a felicity and aptitude which the fainter powers of language can only follow at an immeasurable distance ! Let but my fair pupil rest her hope of a happy destiny on realization of the ideal of art, and the merchant's son will look up with faltering admiration to one who may hold princes captive at her feet !"

Constance promised he should have no reason to regret the pains taken with his grateful pupil, and suddenly changing the subject, remarked on the error he was guilty of, in construing the object of childish friendship into a professed lover. He replied that she had, herself, assigned separation as the origin of her melancholy. If it were not so, he was prepared to listen to a second confession—it was but to fancy the carriage rolling over the stones, the confessional box at the Carmelites, and she might speak unreservedly. It was too dark to perceive her blushes.

"Another day, Monsieur !" uttered Constance drily.

CHAPTER II.

WHATEVER should prove the eventual destiny of Constance, it was sadly apparent that she must undergo a severe ordeal ere reaching the envied station predicted by the professor. Her first misfortune was his unexpected decease. He was cut off suddenly, lamenting his inability to complete an elaborate treatise on the Terpsichorean art. Dying of an epidemic which raged in Paris and the suburbs, he bequeathed a small legacy to Constance, recommending, with his latest breath, that, being for the future her own mistress, his pupil should not permit herself to be carried away, too early, by popular applause, but continue the same strict routine of training ; and, on the stage, retain the same subordinate parts hitherto allotted. Let her competitors st ll keep the start, and indulge the hope for a while, of superiority, till her training, being matured and perfected, she might, with one effort, win the goal at a bound.

The director dead, the griping uncle was overjoyed at the prospect of a rich harvest. It was a common remark, in professional circles, that Constance was designedly kept back by the master of the ballet; that she had capabilities of making an extraordinary sensation; and that his motives, moreover, were selfish. But these reports were unjust. There may be faultiness in excessive training—it may be carried too far—and (through injudicious enthusiasm) beyond the necessary period of probation; but, in the instance of our heroine, the master's intentions were at least pure and disinterested. If his detractors had reflected, that, by the terms of Constance Le Raincy's engagement, all her earnings at the Academie Royale, beyond a fixed allowance for maintenance, accrued to the professor, they must have felt conscious of the injustice of the accusation, as it was the direct interest of a mercenary master to push a pupil to the utmost verge of display and publicity, to make a market of her gains.

But to this selfish intent—although the calumniated professor had acted a noble part—the uncle bent his avaricious views.

The wish of both mother and daughter was to quit the abode of their unfeeling kinsman, and dwell by themselves—a consummation of which they had lived in hope through many a dreary year. On hinting their intention, the music-seller was furious; threatened law-proceedings in sundry shapes and courts; and exhibited a bill of monstrous length and of exorbitant amount, for the board and maintenance of Mrs. Le Raincy and Constance, from the period of arrival in Paris, although the poor lady, during the whole term, had worked hard, beyond her strength, far overpaying the slender charges incurred on her account. The charge for maintenance of the daughter was even more inconsistent, as he had been in receipt of the larger half of her allowance.

In the midst of these vexations, the poor girl sustained a second shock, more painful than the loss of the professor, by the death of Mrs. Le Raincy, which was hastened, if not compassed by the cruel usage of the music-seller. She had been sinking yearly, though her spirits were buoyed up by prospect of a happier period. The certainty of fresh trouble, perhaps a long and harassing law-suit, at the very season when she fondly believed herself and her daughter free from a tyranny of many years' duration, doubtless accelerated the crisis.

The death of Mrs. Le Raincy frustrated the uncle's hopes of immediate gain. A decent interval must, of course, necessarily elapse ere Constance could, with propriety, appear in public; but though the stage was, for the present, forbidden, there was no reason, he remarked, that the pupil should delay making a prospective engagement. With intent that she should adopt his views, he pointed out what steps were essential in order to make a good bargain with the management of the Academie; what amount she might accept, what refuse; matters which, from long connection with operatic professionals, he was far from ignorant of. But when he found her invariably heedless, or inattentive, or, as often happened when he broached the subject—in tears, he changed his tone, accused her of a desire to live in idleness at his expense, and declared that he would conclude a negotiation himself.

Forced, at length, by importunities, and threats of resorting to unpleasant measures, to explain herself fully, she declared her intentions were, in compliance with the dying advice of the professor, to study for a while under the eye of his successor. On hearing this declaration, the rage of the music-seller knew no bounds; the paroxysm of anger into which he was thrown, and the dreadful expressions to which he gave vent, displayed the mean, avaricious, and remorseless spirit of the man in the most forcible colours.

A few days after this altercation, Le Raincy, with a scornful, sneering air of triumph, produced from his pocket a parchment document, which he handed to Constance for perusal. It was the counterpart of an agreement between the management of the Academie Royal and Jaques Le Raincy, Jun., and in behalf of his niece and ward, Constance Le Raincy. The stipulations were duly set forth, as usual in documents of the kind; and penalties for non-performance (binding on both parties) duly enumerated. As Le Raincy was accounted her legal guardian, and had exercised the authority in framing the engagement with the deceased professor, his signature was accepted by the Academie as conveying the full consent of his niece.

This high-handed proceeding excited both dismay and indignation. Had he acted with more craft and less violence, it is probable that the friendless damsel would have submitted to fulfil what his avarice exacted.

But such gross tyranny—such a deep and bitter insult—awoke the long dormant spirit of resistance. The arrogant presumption that she would submit to have her services sold, without having, herself, a voice in the bargain; was too galling to be endured! Could the spirit of her deceased mother—of the lamented and kind-hearted professor—be witnesses to her submission to the degrading contract, would they not contemn her weakness? Must not even her uncle despise, whilst he oppressed her?

Glowing with such thoughts, she summoned courage to tell her harsh kinsman, that the agreement was not binding on one who was her own mistress; and that, for his own sake, he had better take immediate steps to have it cancelled.

"*Parbleu !* mademoiselle," exclaimed Le Raincy, with a sneer, "courage is a virtue of high metal. From whence was it plucked?"

Constance replied that she derived it from a deep sense of the rectitude of her intentions. Were there no other motive for declining the engagement, the circumstance of her being ranked as a principal *danseuse*, instead of, what she really was, a pupil, and subordinate artiste, was quite sufficient to make her decline an invidious honour, to which she was totally incompetent; which would justly entail the envy and dislike of the other members of the corps for her presumption, and likewise endanger, by a premature and ill-advised display, the good opinion of the audience and the court.

Le Raincy listened with a sneer. He was happy, he declared, to hear her express so much deference for the good opinion and favour of the public and the court, (words, by the bye, in that age almost synonymous,) as he knew (here he smiled sarcastically,) that she would, after reading the Gazette he had brought home, change opinions with respect to the brilliant career which was opened at the Academie Royal.

"Read that, mademoiselle!" he said, in conclusion, placing before her the paper.

Constance, foreboding evil, yet at a loss to conjecture his meaning, took up the Gazette with trembling hand. The paragraph respecting herself was partly what, in the language of journalists of the present century, would be called, a well-written puff; but with this difference, that there was a demi-official air in the style, perfectly well understood by readers living under a court, to whom the appearance of a new *prima donna*, or *danseuse* was an affair of as much moment as the appointment of a grand chamberlain or minister of state.

The engagement of Mlle. Le Raincy was announced, as also the evening on which she was to make her first appearance in the principal *role* of the ballet. His Majesty and suite, it was intimated, would not be absent on the occasion. A few critical remarks on the peculiar excellencies of the young lady's style wound up the notice.

Constance flung down the Gazette in despair. In doing so, she caught the eye of the music-seller. A smile of gratified malice played over his countenance.

"Mademoiselle understands the meaning of a *lettre-de-cachet*, I presume?"

Constance was not ignorant of the nature of the document alluded to, nor did she mistake the application of her kinsman's remark. A refractory singer, who had displeased the court, on a late occasion, by refusing to sing on the evening when she had been announced, was conveyed to a place of durance through the instrumentality of a *lettre-de-cachet*, and detained till she made humble apology to his Majesty, or the representative of royalty appointed to receive it.

Her uncle, she perceived, had purposely carried matters to such a length, that the consequence of refusal was no longer purely a domestic quarrel, but involved punishment as severe as awaited the *prima donna's* contumacy. By refusing to appear, she was not merely thwarting his selfish hopes, but was grievously disappointing the management, and passing an affront on the court, who would not fail resenting it.

Le Raincy, of course, foresaw the dilemma in which Constance would be placed; and now openly manifested exultation. In proportion to his joy, as deep was the mortification and chagrin of his niece; it seemed as though it were fated that the tie which connected her with an unfeeling, avaricious kinsman should not be broken; that she was destined to remain his victim, do what she might to extricate herself.

Still Constance, though dismayed, was not subdued. Her soul revolted at the tyranny, and she gained strength even from despair. The crisis was one calculated to call forth her energies, or display her weakness; and, fortunately, it drew forth the latent energies of a mind hitherto unconscious of its powers.

Disgusted with Paris, without one friend remaining to sympathise with her sorrows, or aid in removing them—her heart yearned towards England. Perhaps she might renew acquaintance with the playmate of her childhood; at least it was a pleasant dream to indulge in, even though Arthur Edmonstone should prove as cold and selfish as the world which now environed her; but even were he dead, or living in a distant land, England was the home of her infancy; and the freedom of its institutions, of which she could claim the privileges of a native born subject, promised far superior protection than the despotic interference of the French court, with which she was threatened by her finessing kinsman.

But how accomplish the journey, or, rather, how contrive escape from Paris, for, view it as she may, she could not disguise from herself, that she was a prisoner.

On the eve of her debut as a leading star of the ballet—a danseuse who had excited the expectations of the court—it was in vain to imagine that a passport to the frontiers would be granted; nay the slightest suspicion, on the part of her uncle, the management of the *Academie*, or the court dignitaries, that she meditated flight would cause immediate issue of the dreaded *lettre de cachet.*

It was necessary therefore, to dissemble. The practice was new, and she found herself far from proficient. With hesitation, she asked when it was expected that she should appear at rehearsal.

"To-morrow, at eleven," was the reply.

"To-morrow?" echoed Constance, "impossible!"

"Why?" demanded the uncle with rising fury.

She had no becoming apparel—none but mourning garments—which, for her dear mother's sake, should never be seen within the walls of the *Academie*—she would (the maiden added) die first!

This was a stroke of duplicity, for which the lady must stand excused, and dissimulation was the only weapon now available to defeat her uncle's machinations. Her plea rather softened him. He expected her obstinacy would extend to refusing altogether to attend rehearsal, and was agreeably surprised that her objections were so easily remediable. There were twenty-four hours good, he replied; sufficient time, with proper assistance, to prepare for appearance, in whatever she preferred. And, for the means, if her purse were empty, there was (pulling out his gold) plenty at her disposal.

Constance was obliged to accept the money, or she might have defeated her object by creating suspicion. She was afraid, she remarked, that the rehearsal must be deferred, as she would have to sit up late to aid the modiste in completing her dress, and might be too fatigued to undertake any part in the rehearsal.

Le Raincy, who was altogether unprepared for the courageous attempt which Constance meditated, and who beheld only in her acquiescence, the dread of a young maiden of the horrors of the Conciergerie, or the Bastile, felt very anxious to smooth all lesser difficulties. He would excuse her company, he said, both at the dinner and supper-table; she could keep to her own chamber; and though she might work la   nd were even fatigued on the morrow, he did not expect, that on a first appearance, more would be done at the Academie than assigning to each artiste the *role.*

She was then mistress of herself for the entire day; the very point she was desirous to gain, though her young mind felt a tinge of unhappiness through having resorted to duplicity.

The joy of the music-seller was excessive. He had encountered less trouble than he expected, and already began to indulge in dreams of wealth, flowing from the efforts of Constance. Pecuniary considerations apart, his vanity was also

CONSTANCE APPLIES FOR A PASSPORT TO CALAIS.

flattered with the consideration which must attach to the guardian and protector of the leading *danseuse* in France, nay, in Europe.

Constance was now nearly nineteen, and the *tout-ensemble* of her appearance realized the early anticipations of the deceased enthusiast. Her complexion clear and brilliant, yet of softened lustre; eyes of dewy light, rather than piercing brightness, a form slenderly graceful, and step which enraptured the votary of the ballet, she gleamed on the gay, dissipated, voluptuous audience like an ocean-naiad, new-risen from the deep. Her *tournure*, alone, justified the management

No. 2.

in consenting to the high salary which her uncle demanded; but it was believed, from the style in which she executed the very few *pas-de-seul*, which the restraining system of the late professor permitted, that she would prove the most graceful, if not agile, *danseuse* of the age.

CHAPTER III.

CONSTANCE hastened to secure the legacy bequeathed by the professor. The law's delay had, in the first instance, prevented her receiving it; and of late, she had abstained from inquiry, or pursuit, being far from anxious to make herself mistress of the bequest, or diligent in seeking it, having a presentiment that on special or insidious pretence, her uncle would claim the use of the money.

But the exigency of the situation now determined Constance to claim payment; and if the delays of the courts were still pleaded, to offer cession of the legacy upon immediate receipt of a certain amount. By the notary, she was received very graciously (which might be owing, she thought, to the gazetted announcement) and informed, that although the money was not yet receivable, yet to oblige mademoiselle, or her uncle, he would advance the entire amount, reimbursing himself, when available from the estate. No offer was ever more opportune, or more thankfully received. The worthy gentleman proposed to send home the gold, and the receipt in blank, for her signature; but Constance (as the reader may suppose,) had weighty reasons for declining the notary's politeness.

She was about (she said) to re-appear on the boards of the *Academie Royale*. At the bare mention of this topic, Constance was interrupted by the worthy functionary, who assuming an air of gallantry, declared that her expected *début* was known everywhere; and that he was specially fortunate in having the opportunity of offering his congratulations.

After suitable reply, our heroine stated, that certain purchases were requisite—that a rehearsal was appointed for the morrow—and as he had so kindly offered to forestall the tardy operations of the courts, there was no impediment, she hoped, to transacting the business on the spot. None, whatever! was the ready reply, accompanied by a very low bow, implying how much the notary was honoured by having the chance of obliging mademoiselle.

Constance, after subscribing her name, carried away the gold. The flattering attentions, and empressment of the notary, brought forcibly to mind the remarks of her deceased friend;—the world was indeed at her feet! But how grieved the kind-hearted donor, could he have known that his favorite pupil was reduced to such strait, that her sole hope of escaping from undeserved misery, rested on her securing his bequest! A tear of gratitude trembled on her dark eye-lash. In silence she offered a heart-felt prayer for his soul's health, in which was joined the name of her dear mother.

But there is much yet to accomplish, fair orphan! Many steps of doubt, hazard and peril, lie between thee and the land thou seekest! But courage! the first point is gained, though the goal be not yet won.

Prudence suggested, that before applying for a passport at the bureau, she should make some charge of apparel, to lessen the chance of being recognized. With this view, she hastened home, and attired herself after the style of young girls who earn a livelihood in the shops of milliners and modistes—which her knowledge of stage-effect enabled her to select and adapt with facility. In this guise she presented herself.

In the antechamber were several people awaiting their turn of audience. Constance was about to take a seat near them, when a gentleman, with papers in his hand, in the act of passing to the inner apartment, beheld the new visitor, and appeared struck with her beauty. After a moment's steady gaze, he invited her into the chamber of the bureau, and motioning her to a chair, seated himself at the board, beside an elderly gentleman. Poor Constance, afraid (from this mark of courtesy) that she was known, trembled with apprehension, scarcely venturing to take her eyes from the floor. Soon as the party then occupying the attention of the officials was dismissed, the danseuse was requested to step forward.

The gentleman to whom she was indebted for precedence was a gallant of thirty, or thirty-two, dressed in the height of the luxurious, and gaudy fashion of the period. His fellow-commissioner was apparently of the same station in society, though dressed more soberly, as became maturer age.

The junior with a smile of mingled familiarity and impertinence, (which though effacing her terror of being discovered, was both distressing and offensive,) requested she would communicate her business, It was made known in very few words—she required a passport to Calais, as she was on the point of undertaking a journey to London. "To London!" exclaimed the younger official with affected surprise; "for what purpose?"

Constance did not expect to be catechised on her motives, and though she could not help fancying that the question was prompted rather by private curiosity than routine of duty, though it prudent not to exhibit unwillingness to answer questions. She replied, that she was engaged, as an assistant to a Parisian milliner, established in London.

"Your name, mademoiselle!" asked the old gentleman, at the same time making preparation to fill up a blank passport.

Constance, of course, had no intention to take out a pass in her own name; yet in the hurry of events, confusion of mind, and mingling of hopes and fears, she had delayed preparing herself in this particular, and in consequence, was at a loss how to answer the inquiry.

"Mademoiselle cannot have the passport without furnishing her name," said the elder commissioner, smiling, whilst his pen paused over the printed form.

"Jeanne Dupont," uttered Constance, with hesitating voice and suffused, tingling cheeks.

The name had caught her eye that morning, over the door of a rope-maker's in a by-street, on the way to the notary's, and now suggested itself for the want' of a better.

"And place of abode?" added the junior commissioner.

Constance felt that she was in a dilemma, do what she might, so gave the name of a street in which the said Jeanne Dupont resided—the number she could only guess at. It was obviously the business of the elder gentleman to fill in the address, both in the passport and registry; but she remarked, with alarm, that the junior made a minute of both, which he consigned to his pocket.

Constance was glad to take possession of the document, and hurry from the bureau, glad once more to find herself in the street. She had narrowly, as she imagined, escaped detection; nor indeed was the risk over, as the younger official had obviously a motive in his inquiries, which, whether prompted by conscientious desire of faithfully discharging the duties of his office, or by private sinister design, boded our heroine no good. Whilst reflecting on his behaviour, a hasty step caused her to start—and the commissioner was at her side!

"You walk quick," said he, almost out of breath, "and yet with grace, like one trained to it."

"I have many affairs to attend to," replied the damsel, "Monsieur must excuse my haste."

This was intended as an adieu, as she immediately quickened her pace, with intention of outstripping her unwelcome acquaintance. But the latter was not easily foiled.

"Stay! mademoiselle!" he cried in a loud haughty tone, "we do not let off so easily a young bourgeoise making the trip to England."

"Then I will walk back to the bureau," replied Constance, with an indignation which she in vain strove to suppress.

"Pardon! pardon! Mademoiselle La Fierte!" rejoined the commissioner, planting himself in her way, and laughing the while, "your business at the bureau is concluded—but tell me, when do you start for England?"

Constance was now assured that his purpose, though base, was in no way connected with official station; yet, as she had given a false name and address, discovery would throw her in his power. It were better policy, therefore, to temporize than to fling down defiance. Her purpose was to start immediately, but she adroitly answered, that she should not commence the journey before Saturday night.

"Only three days more to stay in *la grande ville!*" uttered the gallant, in rather lachrymose strain. "And has Paris lost its charm for so pretty a demoiselle?" continued he, in gayer mood; "can nothing tempt mademoiselle to remain? I will, and must have. an interview, if it be only to convince her, that I have an offer to make, more brilliant that any fortune she may obtain in such a triste and silly place as London."

"Monsieur must leave me," exclaimed Constance in a tone of great distress, "or I shall be forced to claim protection from my friends."

She was painfully conscious that they were both observed by passengers. The circumstance of a fine, showy gentleman of quantity—as his dress and appearance indicated—conversing with a young girl of the bourgeoise class, was too striking to escape notice, and doubtless occasioned much comment and witticism. The official was himself sensible of the impropriety, and remarked that the place was far too public for conversation, yet he would only quit her on one condition, that she granted an interview elsewhere.

What should she do? She had commenced the day with deceptive practices which already perilously embrassed her, yet—there was no help for it—she must continue the same path. By pretending to be what she was not, she had put herself out of the pale of ordinary protection. Were she to appeal from the commissioner's insolent importunities to chance passenger, shopkeeper, or other quarter, the affair would, of course reach her uncle's ears; and (other momentous considerations apart) how could she explain satisfactorily, with due regard to her character, her present disguise, for she could call it nothing else?

It were, therefore, less hazardous she deemed, to clear herself from the dilemma by unaided efforts. She trusted that rectitude of conduct would save her, in future from a similar predicament.

If he had aught to say, remarked Constance, which it behoved her to hear, and which was becoming in her to listen to—she should have charge of her mother's wareroom to-morrow afternoon at four o'clock—and he had better come as though he were a customer.

The delighted gallant, enraptured with her frankness, promised punctuality, and —to the lady's great relief—disappeared, whispering a thousand fond adieus. Throughout the morning's adventures, Constance stilled the qualms of conscience by persuading herself that the end justified the means; but the severe lesson which she had just received—the tribulation from which she barely escaped— taught her that deviation from truth, in any cause, for whatever object was fraught with peril, from which extrication might be impossible.

Having rid herself—by an artifice probably suggested by histrionic reminiscences, —of her importunate admirer, Constance next inquired the way to the *Messagerie* or inn-yard, whence started the Calais diligence. Nine o'clock that same evening was the time appointed at which the huge machine would be put in motion. After her passport was carefully inspected by the clerk, and not before, was she permitted to secure, and pay for, a place in the vehicle.

Returning home, she told her uncle's servant, (an ill-grained, unsocial woman, of middle age, in whom she could place no confidence,) that for the remainder of the day, and greater part of the night she should be engaged in her own chamber, preparing, with aid of the *modiste*, a new dress for reappearance at the *Academie*, —and that it was her uncle's special request that she should be denied to all visitors, and neither disturbed nor intruded on.

Having locked the door, Constance, with palpitating heart, sat down to consider what should be the next step. That huge diligence, she reflected, could move but slowly, and were her flight and destination discovered, she might be overtaken by courier, or express-riders, before reaching Calais, or even after arrival, for she was not beyond danger till the packet sailed. To employ porter or lacquey to remove her trunks to the *Messagerie*, though performed unseen by her uncle, or any one in the house, would yet be leaving behind a witness, who might betray the destination of the fugitive. She must, therefore, abandon what she could not carry by hand. It were better incur such a loss than run the risk which the alternative proposed. Her mother's jewellery and her own, occupied but small compass; the professor's legacy (in gold coin) was equally portable, and would provide in London what she was deficient of, or had abandoned; and of apparel, she could carry from the house as much as might serve immediate exigencies. To baffle the music-seller as to the rout taken, after her flight was discovered, was more difficult, and she could not devise any scheme which promised success.

In the meantime, Constance kept the chamber door locked, lest it were discovered by unlucky chance or *contretemps*, that she was alone, instead of aiding the *modiste*. It is the usual style in Paris, for a family to occupy an extended floor, or suite of rooms, more or less in number, according to circumstances; whence it happens that saloon, sleeping-chambeer, and domestic offices approximate very closely. The designs of Constance were much favoured by a departure from the customary plan. The music-seller occupied a *boutique*, or shop, opening on the street, a kitchen beneath, with other rooms on the floor above the shop. Hence our heroine was free from the prying eyes of the servant, and by carrying with her own hands (much to the crabbed woman's delight) the dinner-tray to her chamber, preserved the seclusion she so much coveted.

As day declined, her courage grew apace, and she ventured twice to the *Messagerie*, carrying each time, under her mantle, a small trunk or box, by which means a larger portion of apparel was removed than she had promised herself.

But the chief difficulty remained. As she saw her trunks lifted to the roof of the ponderous vehicle, she despaired of ever escaping from France by such a slow conveyance. Her uncle, she was sure, would be joined by the directory of the Academie and by the government, in taking every possible steps to capture the audacious runaway.

But devise some scheme she must—and it was a shame, she deemed, that an histrionic artiste should be so baffled. Her mother's family were originally settled at Marseilles. It were possible and feasible, that though some members were slaughtered, and others escaped from France—on the revocation of the edict of Nantes—yet a more fortunate branch remained and prospered; and to look for protection in such a quarter was an idea likely to be entertained by an orphan in the oppressed condition of Constance. Why should she not, therefore make Le Raincy believe that she had fled to the south?

As no better idea presented, and the time began to draw near, Constance hurried to a *Messagerie*, from which the southern diligence started. It left the yard, as she found on inquiry, at an early hour in the morning. Our adventurous heroine growing bold by practice, requested a place to be registered in the name of Constance Martigny—the latter being the name of her mother's family. Difficulty was started in the absence of a passport, an omission which the lady accounted for by stating, that the journey was to be undertaken by her cousin, residing at Charenton, at which town she would take possession of her seat.

"Then why not make the registry at Charenton?" demanded the clerk.

She had no better reply, than that her cousin was fearful that all the places might be taken in Paris, and on the arrival of the diligence at Charenton be disappointed in her intended journey, The excuse, greatly to our heroine's relief, was deemed satisfactory, and the name of Constance Martigny registered, and part of the fare paid.

On return, Constance took occasion, whilst in the kitchen, to inquire of her uncle's servant at what town the Marseilles diligence would halt to allow the passengers to dine. As our heroine expected, the woman expressed surprise at the question, and asked the motive of the inquiry, which Constance in the first instance evaded, but after some demur, said that the modiste, now working in her chamber, was on the point of undertaking the journey, and they had been chatting together about it.

The conversation then dropped, and Constance retired, trusting that when her flight was discovered, pursuit would be made in the direction of Marseilles.

As nine o'clock drew near, the courage of our heroine wavered. Having completed every preliminary, the mind was thrown on itself, with leisure to reflect on the manifold dangers which the enterprise presented. She was forsaking home, profession, and prospects—most flattering in all eyes save her own—for a land where she was unknown, her parents, perhaps, forgotten; where, destitute of protection, she must run every risk encountered by a lone female in seeking to establish a livelihood. The annoyance she experienced that very day exemplified what she might expect in future, with the additional risk, that in a foreign country, she had no refuge, no friendly arm to fly to, or evoke.

Yet the dreaded alternative ! She could not brook living the slave of her uncle. Her mother's untimely death made his very image odious to her—even Paris itself, with its gaieties and courtly splendour, proved a forlorn and bitter spot since her bereavement. To remain was moral suffocation. Like the solitary, imprisoned bird, whose mate has expired, she panted to breathe other air, where she might forget her wrongs, and her grief.

But what says the hand of the dial. There remained but fifteen minutes ! The die is cast, she will go ! Praying the intercession of the Virgin—beseeching the prayers of her dear mother, whose memory was sweetly, yet mournfully linked with the chamber which she now prepares to quit for ever—Constance, with trembling hand, removes from the mantel the cross, beneath which she has so oft knelt in meditation. This, with a miniature portrait of her parent, are all she removes from the walls. The lamp is trimmed and left burning on the table, After casting one more hurried glance around, she locks the door, places the key in her bosom, and stealing down stairs, escapes unperceived into the street.

In the Messagerie she finds the huge diligence already harnessed to a team of horses. The clerk calls out successively the names of the passengers. *Jeanne Duponte !* is shouted.

"I am here," replied Constance.

She is handed into the vehicle, already nearly full. There are people to the right and the left, and on the long seat opposite, but she cannot recognize their faces in the gloom. She shuts her eyes, and leans backward, resigned to whatever may befall.

The wooden boots of the postilion clank on the sharp pointed stones, and as the rolling mass emerges from the dark archway of the Messagerie, his knotted whip—to the fancy of our heroine, cracks adieu to Paris.

CHAPTER IV.

OVER the roughly-paved streets the diligence was rolled, groaning and staggering beneath its superincumbent weight, till, joyful event ! the barriers were passed. Now jostled against the shoulder of her left hand companion, and, anon, thrown in a contrary direction, unconscious of the name, rank, occupation nay, the very sex of the passenger on either side ; so dark was the interior of the diligence, so enveloped in cloak, mantle and roquelaure were the night-travellers by whom our heroine was surrounded.

Scope for speculation was there of the scene which morning would disclose ; but the mind of Constance had other material to feed on. And yet, spite of gloomy reflections, and oft-recurring presages of misfortune, she was not wholly insensible to the novelty, even the romance, of her situation. Cosily ensconsed among unknown companions, her mind, at intervals, dismissed its terrors, and revelled in a feeling of security. How could the famed *debutante* of the *Academie Royale* be detected beneath her mantle in the dark corner of a Calais diligence. Sometimes, (as the current of fancy changed,) with strained gaze, she would endeavour to pierce the gloom, and picture the features of the passengers , and then, with closed eyes, she would relapse into mournful reverie.

Broken slumbers visited her eyelids, and she dreamed frightful visions—that she was imprisoned in the conciergerie, and each public night of the Academie led to the stage, to receive rough tribute of hissing and maledictions, from whence she was reconducted to her prison-chamber.

In the middle of the night the dark walls and bars of the visionary gaol were dispelled by a crashing noise. She awoke and saw that the passengers were, one by one, descending from the diligence. Following their steps, she found herself in the interior of a large inn. Hot coffee, cakes and other refreshments were served, and Constance, for the first time, had opportunity of beholding her companions.

" Did not mademoiselle sit next to me ?" asked a voice from amidst a huge pile of overcoats.

Constance replied that she did not know, though she could find her seat again on the right hand bench.

This short dialogue was overheard by a lady who declared that the questioner was correct in his surmise ; mademoiselle sat next to him and opposite the speaker.

" I would recommend," continued she, " that madamoiselle follow our fashion ; the night is very chilly and will be much colder towards morning."

And ere Constance was aware, or could prevent it, the officious, but kind lady dropped into the maiden's cup a sprinkling of *eau-de-vie.*

In ten minutes the travellers were all reseated, and the diligence, after traversing several ill-lighted streets, passed under the groaning archway of the two-gates. A sweep of the northern blast, from the open country, rushed through the inlets of the vehicle, and gave countenance to the prediction of our heroine's fellow traveller But Constance was now worn out, both in mind and body, by the fatigue which both had experienced through the most trying day of her life, and she fell asleep from which she was only disturbed by the loud conversation of the passengers after day-break.

The lady seated opposite (the same who was disposed to take such good care of herself, and her fellow traveller,) was about five-and-thirty, with some pretensions to beauty, lively in her manners, prompt in discourse. At first, Constance was rather puzzled to determine her situation in society. The face was smooth, unwrinkled and plump, bespeaking good living, and a mind at ease ; but, in the opinion of the damsel, her manner betrayed an entire absence of the proper reserve which should distinguish a lady of family and quality, travelling by public conveyance. But this idea underwent change, after discovering that the female sitting by her side was her servant, or tire woman. Much baggage had she, and, doubtless, of considerable value, if one were to judge from the anxiety occasionally expressed for its safety and proper condition. A lady of rank, thought Constance, perhaps too poor to provide chaise, or separate conveyance, but certainly rather too free spoken.

Madame took much, and kindly notice of Constance, as also did all the passengers, when they found that she was travelling unprotected. Every attention was paid to render her condition comfortable ; and could she have expelled from her imagination the picture of her enraged uncle, armed with the dreaded *lettre-de-cachet*, she might have been happy. But fear of being overtaken made each moment miserable. Though, in reality, she ran as much risk in darkness as by day ; yet night lent a fancied security, which was now thoroughly dispelled. How impatiently bounded her heart whilst she watched the progress of the slowly moving vehicle ; how she longed to accelerate the speed of the flagging horses—how she deprecated the delay in surmounting the steep hill—the time spent in the towns along the route ! In every clatter of a horse's hoof—each rumble of approaching chaise, she fancied her pursuers at hand.

Beholding her distress, though unable to account for it, madame was doubly attentive to the young traveller. On learning that her destination was London, her interest increased ; she was journeying thither herself ; and they might as well, she said, for the remainder of the journey, travel in company.

The maiden gladly acceded to the proposal, though assent was conveyed in the faintest tone, whilst reflecting that the passing hour might be the last spent in the lady's society ; that she might be torn disgracefully, like a criminal, from the good-natured and affable passengers with whom she travelled.

On entering Calais, the crisis of her fate was at hand. Her agitation was extreme, and did not pass unnoticed by madame, but the hurry of events prevented remark or inquiry. At this town the travellers parted company ; several were citizens of Calais ; others were destined to a journey along the coast ; whilst madame, taking in charge her young acquaintance, lost no time in making inquiry respecting the Dover packets.

It was explained, that the captain of a packet was at that time in the hotel, and, though the tide was favourable, he intended lying over four-and-twenty hours, or longer, for chance of more passengers. Madame requested to see him.

"I prefer crossing to-night," said the lady, turning to Constance. Looking at her watch, she added, "and we should reach Dover before midnight—it is now six o'clock."

Constance trembled with delight. She felt that she could have fallen on her knees and besought her to keep in the same mind ; but she knew not how to trust a stranger. What remark she might have uttered was prevented by entry of the captain.

To the surprise of our heroine, the lady asked the captain, in excellent English, when he intended sailing, as she understood both wind and tide served.

When he could obtain a fair complement of passengers—was the man's reply.

Madame asked if he would sail immediately, with what passengers he might have, including herself, and the young French lady in the room, and she would give a certain sum, which she named.

"Not enough," replied the captain, shaking his head. There were only two cabin, and one deck passenger, beside themselves.

"I have baggage !" exclaimed the lady, pointedly and earnestly, "and it would be better to land at night."

It was evident this conversation was intended to be private and confidential ; neither captain nor lady anticipating that the "young French lady" understood what passed. Yet Constance was listening, with intense interest, to the dialogue, and fearing that the negotiation would break off through non-compliance of madame to increase the offer, said, in her native tongue, to which she had long been a stranger, that she would pay the difference, whatever the captain demanded.

"Ah ! miss," cried the master of the packet, "then you have luggage also."

But the lady did not recover from her surprise as readily as the sailor. She was struck dumb. The inhabitants of the respective countries were not so familiar with each other's language in the days of the second George as in the nineteenth century, and this remark is more applicable to the continental nation than the islanders; a French woman speaking English was a rare phenomenon in that age.

The captain appeared to enjoy the joke heartily.

"Come! come!" said he, "I see, if you don't understand each other, you both understand me. If Miss will say five guineas, we'll have the baggage on board in a twinkling. The landlord will take your passports, as I judge the commissioner has gone home."

CONSTANCE MAKES THE ACQUAINTANCE OF MRS. BENNINGTON.

Constance, blushing and confused, offered the money, but the captain said, that when they were on board would be time enough; he must run after his other passengers. And, without waiting reply, he left the room.

"Well! you surprise me!" exclaimed madame, approaching her young friend.

"Had we not better go on board the packet?" asked Constance? "we shall have more leisure, and you shall very readily have my confidence."

"With all my heart," replied the other, laughing merrily.

No. 3.

The captain was a man of his word. The ladies, the maid servant, and the luggage, were speedily embarked; the passports, in absence of the proper authority, being deposited with the landlord of the hotel.

With intense emotion, Constance leaned over the bulwark watching the operations by which the packet was cleared from the harbour. Her fellow-passenger was more busily engaged, being occupied, with her maid, in counting the number of her packages and trunks, which were numerous.

The craft receded from the harbour; the sails filled with the freshening breeze, and Constance and her fortunes were fairly embarked on the ocean. As she watched the gradual recession from the shore, she silently, fervently, breathed a prayer of gratitude and thanks, that she had been permitted to escape.

Leaning over the rail, looking intently through the gloom of early night, at the fading view of land, she suddenly bethought herself of the key of the chamber, in her uncle's house, which she had for ever abandoned. Taking it from her bosom, she committed it to the dark waters; it fell unseen amid the surge. She felt a gentle tap on her shoulder, and, turning, beheld madame.

"Come below," said the lady, "or you will be frozen."

Retiring to the inner cabin, Constance said she was anxious to dispel any unpleasant prejudices which her fellow-traveller entertained on account of her precipitate haste to leave the French territory. She was not flying to avoid the consequences of any misdeed, but to escape the tyrany of a cruel kinsman, And thereupon she narated the brief story of her life, to which the lady listened with much interest.

When Constance finished, her companion said that it was now her turn. They had taken each other for natives of France, out, in fact, were both Englishwomen. Her name was Bennington, She was a milliner of repute, residing in Tavistock-street, London, and had the honour of ranking the queen and the royal family among her customers. In the habit, yearly, of visiting the French metropolis, in order to carry home the newest fashions, she was, (as Miss Le Raincy was aware) much encumbered with luggage, which she found great difficulty in passing through the custom house at Dover : and, by arriving at night, with a little aid from the captain of the packet, and a little money elsewhere bestowed, she saved much trouble, and considerable expense.

Our heroine expressed her happiness in having been so fortunate as to meet with Mrs. Bennington : she could never have summoned courage to induce the captain to put to sea on her own account, and might, but for the happy rencontre, have been at that very hour, under escort of the French police, *en route* to Paris.

Nor need, as Mrs. Bennington observed, her happiness rest with what was past. She was very glad that Miss Le Raincy had made her acquainted with her history and family, as it removed all obstacles to making offer of a home in Tavistock-street. Mr Bennington was a quiet man ; they had no children ; and would both welcome the young lady as a boarder. If her views were professional, she could not be lodged in a more favourable locality, Tavistock-street being the chosen mart of fashion.

Tears were the silent, yet eloquent, reply to the kind offer.

After a pleasant run of a few hours, the packet entered Dover harbour, and Constance stepped on deck to behold her native shore. She was now in safety ! Whatever labour, whatever privations she might, in future, encounter, she felt that her troubles were ended. Hope flattered ; she knew not the future, and was happy.

Mrs. Bennington was successful in clearing her luggage. Places were taken in the London stage, which was to start next morning, and the ladies retired to rest. The ensuing day they pursued their journey, and, eventually, without further peril or adventure, the court-milliner and her interesting guest were safely housed in Tavistock-street.

CHAPTER V.

Two weeks passed very swiftly in her new home without attempt, on the part of Constance, to resume either the discipline or duties of her old profession, or to choose a new one. She was indeed so very happy that mere existence seemed a blessing. Mr. Bennington proved as amiable and considerate as his wife reported; the latter was kindness personified, though shrewd, persevering, and possessing a keen eye to her own advantage.

Gently, she awoke Constance from her dream; reminded her that she was gifted with an accomplishment as highly esteemed in London as in Paris; and that the opera season had commenced. These hints were kindly received by our heroine; she had not forgotten, she declared, that she was a pupil of promise, and the prophecy of her late master she was determined to verify—yet she dreaded the ordeal, and yet more, she dreaded an interview with the manager—persons of his station were, in general, so cold, heartless and indifferent.

Mrs. Bennington urged that, however coldly she might be received by the manager, the public would receive a lady of her talents with warmth and rapture; and from all that she knew of the present condition of the ballet-corps, she had but little to fear on the score of competition.

But Constance, though conscious of superior talents, was distrustful of her reception, and could not summon courage to present herself to the manager, till she witnessed the performance of the corps. The accomplishment of her wish she resolved to unite with a pleasant surprise to the Benningtons, in return for manifold civilities. Unknown to them, she hired a box, for an evening when she was certain they were disengaged.

"How unexpected!" exclaimed Mrs. Bennington, when Constance at dinne announced what she had done.

"Nay—what more likely?" observed her spouse. "Miss Le Raincy has proved herself such a thorough adept at stratagem."

The opera was Almahide; the ballet, a production of her poor deceased master. The representation brought tears to her eyes, not certainly chargeable to the pathos of the incidents; but the scenes recalled forcibly the instructions of the professor —even the very words of commendation and reproof which he used at rehearsal were associated with the turns and shifting display of scenery and dancing.

The little party returned home extremely well pleased; the Benningtons, inasmuch as they found themselves in company of so many of their titled and aristocratic customers, whose costume they were better able to criticise, than the merit of Italian airs and recitative, or the agile and graceful *tours* of the dancers—and Constance was all the happier, as her fears were lulled after witnessing the performance of her rivals in expectancy.

In that age, as in the present, the Italian opera house was situate in the Haymarket. Thither Constance repaired next morning, much to the gratification of the Benningtons, who were anxious to see their young friend occupy a distinguished statiou.

Our *danseuse* had certainly imbibed a considerable portion of her master's system with respect to the conduct and management of professional skill. There might be vanity, perhaps coquetry, in the quiet unobtrusive mode adopted of seeking an engagement with the great autocrat of the Haymarket. She had been taught to surprise by displays of unexpected talent, rather than aim at exciting keen expectation which possibly she might disappoint. The latter system, (as she was instructed,) may perhaps suit the management by drawing full houses, but it should ever be an object with the artist to surpass, rather than only equal, or perhaps fall short of ardent curiosity and excitement. It is wise to leave an unoccupied corner of the admiration of an audience wherein to win new laurels and trophies.

Without introduction, previous communication, or transmitted memorial conveying statements of what might be expected from a promising pupil of the *Academie,* she simply requested an interview with the manager. After several hours delay, the request was fortunately granted—it was her beauty which gained access to the —in general—most inaccessible of men.

A manager is either all warmth or all indifference. Eager in search of novelty, of anything with semblance of attraction, he is careless to appeals from parties, or quarters, owning no extrinsic excellence, or adventitious reputation of an *ad captandum* character, to allure the public.

The magnate of the opera was very polite; invited her to a seat, and threw himself into an *ex-officio* chair of ample dimensions. His left hand hung over the side, twirling between the fingers, his Ramilies cocked-hat, which spun round and round on the carpet, on its longest point, like a teetotum. In this easy posture, assumed as an air of careless dignity, after one indolent glance at the fair visitor, he had already—in his own idea—settled her pretensions. The face was uncommonly handsome, the figure slender; both good theatrical qualities—and were she stupid and lazy as an owl, she was at any rate, worth so many shillings per week, to occupy a prominent station in the grouping of the classic, or chivalric ballet.

"And your name, mistress, is Le Raincy—a good name for a play-bill—but you are English, if I mistake not, by your speech—are you not?"

Constance replied in the affirmative.

"And you would join our corps-de-ballet?" continued the manager, "the English never take in that department, even if they happen to turn out pretty dancers. In a generation or two, when the ballet is better understood here, we may perhap look for a growth of native artists."

Pausing a few moments, he at length said, that as she professed to have undergone considerable discipline and training by a French master, he would engage her, without trial, to take station among the *coryphees* —meaning those who dance in groups—and that her own merit, whatever it might be, would bring her forward to a more prominent position in due time.

"Your system of management, sir," replied Constance gravely, "I cannot but approve of; it partakes of the spirit of my late master's instructions. His advice was, never to heed—even if your talents were superior—being placed at bottom of the class, for merit would soon obtain ascendancy. If this be your system, sir, with the ballet-corps of the king's opera—that all engage without trial, and find their level afterward, I shall be happy and ready to join it on such terms."

"And on what other terms could you join it, mistress?" asked the manager, looking more serious, and spinning the hat much slower.

"Monsieur Le Voisin—did he enter the corps after the fashion you propose?" asked the *danseuse.*

The manager admitted that he did not; but then Le Voisin, before he engaged, had the *eclat* which attaches to a pupil of the late esteemed director of the ballet-corps at Paris, and he had been much applauded even on the French boards.

"And so have I," said Constance.

"The d—l you have!" exclaimed the magnate, starting with an energy which caused his Ramilies to pirouette along the carpet, "but tell me really what you can do—what your standing is in the profession?"

Constance affirmed that she had executed a *pas-de-seul* before the assembled court, which elicited the applause of royalty. She admitted that it was a solitary feat, and was not followed by a second attempt.

"And why?" asked the manager.

Our *danseuse* confessed that it was because the director would not permit the display on a second occasion.

'He had good reason, mistress," observed the autocrat with a sagacious shake of the head, "a single swallow does not make a summer ; and a solitary *pas-de-seul* does not give the standing of a principal *danseuse*. Your history would imply, that opportunity has been afforded—the attempt made—and you failed—retiring to your original position. The refusal of the director to allow the experiment being repeated in the person of his own pupil, is tolerably convincing of his estimation of her abilities."

This was a turn in the argument which made poor Constance bite her lips with vexation. Her previous vantage-ground of quiet irony was cut away by the harsh, and it must be confessed, specious remark. She felt that it would be useless to attempt explaining how highly her deceased friend commended the display in question , and that it was through his certainty of her attaining a distinguished eminence that he would not permit her—at what he deemed too early an age—to be flattered, and perhaps, in consequence, seduced from severe discipline and training, by popular applause. To extenuate on this point, she felt were to pour idle words into the ear of a London manager priding himself on shrewdness. And thus she stood condemned by the misconstrued act of him who had her welfare so much at heart!

Constance was disconcerted ; her pride humbled, and—as she could not but confess—very justly humbled. She had sought an interview in a spirit of proud humility, maintained the argument with sarcasm, which though quiet, was not less intended to convey reproof, and behold ! her expected triumph was dissipated. His friendly remonstrance, on perceiving her vexation, added bitterness to the defeat. He bade her not be discouraged. She had a figure and a face, sure to be applauded, whatever might be thought of her dancing—and concluded by saying, that he should be happy to see her the same hour to-morrow, and would, in the meanwhile, consider how he could best make use of her services.

The young traveller returned home sadly humiliated by the disappointment. It is on such occasions as these, when we have met repulse in a quarter to which we fondly looked for preferment, that we think meanly of our faculties, fancy that we have over-estimated our abilities, mistaken our natural aim and scope. The future presents nought but a dreary blank, whilst the baffled, wounded spirit seeks mournful consolation in brooding over half-forgotten sorrows and wounds, which time had well-nigh healed.

Constance, in the solitude of her chamber, wept the night through, lamenting the loss of her dear parent so suddenly snatched away. Who would have consoled her under drear loss of hope like her poor mother ? When the violence of these thoughts were subdued, by unrestrained excess, her mind wandered back to the scenes of childhood with the vain wish that she could retreat into herself, be again what she then was, and dwell once more amid the sweet thoughts and happy influences which haunted her the day long, when her playmate Arthur, and the narrow circuit of their gardens was world wide enough for happiness.

And where now was Arthur, who should have welcomed her to their native land ? Alas ! he was no longer the Arthur, even as she had ceased to be, the Constance of childhood. Young Edmonstone, if he still lived, might regard his former play-mate coldly—nay, perhaps, if they met, she herself might take a dislike. They would not recognize each other—they were both changed—his very features were almost forgotten. Why dwell on the hope of again meeting her playmate ? Rather let his image be enshrined amid the bright undying tints which dwell in memory's chamber, than seek to break the charm by encountering a cold, perhaps repulsive, reception, from a gay prosperous youth who would hold lightly the advances to renewed friendship of a friendless, solitary orphan like herself !

Toward morning, Constance fell into a deep slumber, and slept till the loud jarring of carriage-wheels, thundering peals performed on knockers by comely foot-man, or slim, woolly-headed negro-page—slamming of coach-steps and doors, and all the manifold tokens of London being awake and abroad, caused our sorrowing *danseuse* to start from her dreams. She flew to the window. Tavistock-street—

now so quiet and deserted, with its bookseller's shops, and nearly unpeopled cause-way—was then ringing with the discordant melody of fashionable life. It was indeed very late—she must have sadly overslept herself! But why did not Mrs. Bennington summon her, as usual, to breakfast?

On descending, she was complimented by the milliner on the soundness of her slumbers; the servant had failed waking her, although she knocked at the door louder than ordinary. Mr. Bennington had gone to the city, two hours ago, and since his departure, a maid of honour came from St. James's, and carried to the palace an assortment of merchandise for the Queen's inspection; so that, as Mrs. Bennington observed, Constance had narrowly missed seeing her majesty, by lying in bed, as the royal personage usually came herself, and minutely inspected the show-rooms after recent importations, but was that morning indisposed.

"Then there is a point of sympathy between us," remarked Constance, "for I was unwell—but I perceive it is near the hour of my interview with the manager, though I am afraid I shall make but a poor bargain on a fast-day."

The lady would not hear of her leaving the house without breakfast; it was but to add coffee to the luncheon now preparing, and Miss Le Raincy would not be detained beyond the time of appointment. The milliner dined at the fashionable hour, three o'clock, for the very cogent reason, that her noble and aristocratic customers would then be discussing more substantial matters than the trimmings of a bonnet. But the good lady had to talk so much, and so fast, deliver so many extempore essays on taste and the fine arts—of Tavistock-street,—that she was exhausted long before dinner time, and each day, during the busy season, stole ten minutes for a slight refection; and to which she now invited Constance.

"There are five minutes more, good," exclaimed Mrs. Bennington, preventing her friend rising. "You shall attend on the manager in becoming style this morning. The Duke of Portland's carriage is at the door, waiting to take home some orders which the girls are packing up. The carriage can set you down at the stage door before driving to Coventry-street for the ladies, who are making a call there."

Constance remonstrated against this arrangement, but the milliner insisted, and declared she should be really angry, if it were refused. She knew London much better than Miss Le Raincy—the circumstance would not fail being reported to the manager, and must have great weight. There could not be the slightest objection to the carriage passing by way of the Haymarket, which was scarcely out of the direct line to Coventry-street and Cavendish-square.

Behold our *danseuse* amidst a gaping throng, attracted to the milliner's door by the splendid liveries, assisted into the carriage with the same ceremony as though she were a fair scion of the illustrious house of Bentinck—passing in such state to visit a manager who the day before proposed an engagement of a few shillings a week.

The carriage drew up with a sharp recoil at the stage entrance, and the knocker thundered so loudly that poor Constance felt ashamed to descend. The coach door opened, and on each side stood a footman with arm extended for support—suggesting to the histrionic fancy of our heroine, the descent of beauty from her magic car. It so happened, that the manager arrived almost at the same moment, and beholding the well-known ducal liveries and blazonry, doubting not that the visit had reference to engagement of an additional box, or other special matter, he flew to assist in the descent. With left arm extended as a pedestal for the momentary pressure of the slender gloved-fingers of the lady, his right hand drew the Ramilies, with a sweep to the very ground, whilst his body describing a similar curve, the point of the sword and huge buckram skirts of the coat were elevated far into the air. The carriage drove off.

It was perhaps fortunate for both parties, in avoiding an untoward scene in the street, that the manager did not venture to look the lady in the face till he ushered her into the vestibule.

"Your Grace will, I hope, do me the honour," began the polite manager, " of stepping to my poor ——"

" The same apartment I saw you in yesterday," cried Constance, who had gained sufficient courage to feel pleasure in revenge for his triumph in the former interview.

" Your Grace ?—no !—yes ! do I dream ? Have I not the honour of speaking to—? By G—d ! madam—whom have I the honour of addressing ?" stammered the bewildered manager, blushing with surprise and vexation. The face and voice were the same he had seen and heard in his parlour, the day previous, but the apparition of the equipage still confused his judgment—made him still doubtful of the true rank of his visitor.

" You are speaking to Constance Le Raincy," said the maiden quietly, " I believe I am not many minutes beyond the hour appointed."

" Yes ! yes !" replied the autocrat hurriedly, as he led the way, without caring to let his face be seen by the fair visitor.

" Well ! mistress !" exclaimed the manager, throwing open the parlour door, and attempting to laugh away his confusion. " I am—and I suppose we are both —the same people we were yesterday."

" There is a mystery about Mademoiselle Le Raincy," continued he, handing Constance a chair, " which I have no privilege or desire to penetrate. I am not merely alluding to the odd *contretemps* which occurred just now—but from what Le Voisin tells me, I believe, I have the pleasure of addressing an *artiste* of much higher pretensions than I had first imagined. Indeed your name is not altogether new to me, but I should have expected a lady from the *Academie Royale* would have been ushered with more formal and precise credentials. This circumstance so far threw me off my guard, that the name made no impression. Still mademoiselle must admit that she has her trophies yet to win."

" And I *will* win them," exclaimed Constance, " though it be without parade or flourish of trumpets."

It was very evident to the *danseuse* that the autocrat had been not only canvassing her abilities with Le Voisin, but also seeking information in other channels, and that he had received an encouraging report.

In course of a confidential conversation, the manager expressed himself with much candour. As Le Raincy, he said, had struck none of the usual notes for taking the town by storm—set afloat no artifices to raise expectation in the public mind, she afforded him no plea to place her above the present ladies of the corps who were eternally quarrelling with him and among themselves, respecting the relative importance and prominence of their *roles*, in every successive ballet, and there were so few passable dancers in London, that he was very much at their mercy To a leading continental reputation, they must of course succumb, but Miss Le Raincy's talents, (which Le Voisin had spoken very highly of) though unequivocal and undoubted, were as yet unknown this side the channel. Were he, even for one night, to assign her the post of *premiere danseuse*, it would—whilst present circumstances forced him to pay such disproportioned homage to mediocrity—raise a hirlwind about his ears, perhaps a mutiny in face of the audience.

Yet for his own sake, he was disposed to offer Miss Le Raincy very fair terms, and as far as he could possibly venture, afford her the opportunity of creating, what he was pleased to call, " a rage" in the *beau monde*. Some means, he said, must be devised to prevent the jealousy of her rivals being awakened till their opposition, or threats, were pointless. If he could only bring matters to pass so as to gain for the *debutante*, possession of the boards, that she might carry the public with her by a brilliant, yet unexpected display, there was nothing more for either manager or performer to dread.

The interview concluded by Constance accepting a very fair conditional agreement, subject to a higher rate of salary, if she won the public favour. He stipulated, and she did not refuse —although she preferred the English appellative— to be announced as Mademoiselle Le Raincy. It was a sacrifice to public prejudice, he said, which for his sake, if not her own, she must submit to.

On taking note of her address, he complimented Constance on the locality. It was, he remarked, judiciously chosen, and augured more for her experience, than he could have expected from her quiet unobtrusive mode of making known her pretensions to a London manager

---

CHAPTER VI.

Our *danseuse* returned home far better pleased than after the first interview. The manager certainly improved on acquaintance; his frankness and candour won her esteem. The Benningtons were equally well delighted with the reception.

"You see," said the milliner, triumphantly, "what the carriage and livery of a duchess can effect."

Constance did not care to reply to her good tempered friend, that the equipage would have proved but of trifling service in riveting an engagement, without the report of Le Voisin, and others, on the extent of her Parisian celebrity. Though the manager, she perceived, was mystified, and doubtless would have liked to put the question, whether she had gained a patroness in such a distinguished quarter— as presumptive evidence warranted—yet he was, she deemed, too much a man of the world to betray intense curiosity, and our heroine had the good sense to be aware, that he would soon unravel the mystery, after being made acquainted with her place of abode.

At breakfast next morning, the good fortune of Constance was once more the theme of conversation. Mr. Bennington observed that his fair friend would now have a busy time of it, and if her *debut* were as triumphantly successful as her friends expected, would find herself way-laid, and her leisure encroached on by a host of idlers.

Constance replied with a smile, that she had no doubt she should find the day not long enough, what with rehearsals and other occupations, and should sometimes envy him his leisure.

"My leisure," he exclaimed in surprise.

"Mr. Bennington's leisure!" echoed his spouse.

It appeared on explanation—to the extreme merriment of the parties concerned —that Constance was under the impression, that the entire labours of the business rested with the lady, and that the gentleman was comparatively an idle man; whereas, as our heroine was given to understand, a considerable portion of each day was spent by Mr. Bennington in city warehouses, making purchases, examining goods, and the remainder of his time in keeping the accounts and books--no trifling duty.

"Miss Le Raincy, has made as great a mistake about my occupations," said the gentleman, smiling at his spouse, "as when she took you for a lady of quality."

"She is not the first that has made the same mistake," replied the wife, colouring, "though when James Bennington is at my side, I admit such a mistake is impossible."

"Adieu !" exclaimed the husband, making his escape.

The ladies had scarcely taken another cup of chocolate ere they were frighted from their propriety by the entrance of no less a personage than the manager.

The great magnate of the Haymarket, emperor of things theatrical, saluted very cordially, the queen of Tavistock-street, arbitress and empress over things fashionable! Perhaps some passing thought of their respective stations crossed his fancy, as he sat down to partake the proffered chocolate.

"We preside over different realms," he remarked to the milliner, "but in the present instance, both lay claim to the same subject." And he glanced at the blushing Constance.

"Mine is the prior claim!" cried the lady.

"Let us divide our rule," rejoined the manager, "I have a strong interest in mademoiselle, and as she is so unprotected——"

"Not unprotected, sir, while Mr. Bennington and myself have the power of affording protection," exclaimed she of Tavistock-street, interrupting the dignitary of the Haymarket.

It was neither the wish nor policy of the manager to give offence.

CONSTANCE IN THE DUCHESS OF PORTLAND'S CARRIAGE VISITS THE MANAGER.

He begged pardon for having used a word which very inadequately conveyed his meaning, which was, that as she had no legal guardian, she might rely, that in all matters relating to her public welfare and reputation, he would endeavour to separate the manager from the friend, and act as far as he could consistently with his interests, a paternal part.

It gave him, he said, extreme pleasure to find mademoiselle domiciled with the Benningtons. There were many matters of domestic propriety and conduct, which as the lady was aware, from her knowledge of London, mademoiselle should be extremely rigid in observing; and whilst he took charge of her

No. 4.

interest with the public, and kept an eye over those who approached her at the theatre and behind the scenes, he felt relieved that a weightier responsibility lay with his good ally of Tavistock street, a lady in every way so competent to the charge.

After these civilities, he proceeded to business-matters, and informed the *debutante* that he had fixed her first appearance for next Saturday evening; and that on Thursday morning, (naming the hour,) if she would be present at rehearsal, he would introduce her to the ladies and gentlemen of the corps, both ballet and musical.

On Thursday the promised introductions took place, and she rehearsed a third-rate part in a ballet of no peculiar interest. The *role* assigned was not only far beneath her merits, but much below the grade of character in which it was intended she should appear. But a *ruse* was necessary, in order to defeat the jealous machinations of rivals, and the success which both the manager and our heroine confidently anticipated from the manœuvre, reconciled Constance to the humble part. But though the ruler of the opera escaped the rebellion which awaited, had he dared assign Le Raincy what he really intended she should fill, the principal *role*, yet the marked personal attention he paid to the new figurante did not escape notice. As his politeness could not be accounted homage to the talents and re-nown of the *debutante*, more dishonourable motives were suggested, not discoun-tenanced by the attractive form and beauty of Constance. Many were the illiberal sneers and inuendoes indulged in by her rivals, but happily for her peace of mind they were unheard.

As previously arranged, a secret meeting took place, after rehearsal in the mana-ger's parlour. There were present the great autocrat, our heroine, the leader of the orchestra, and Le Voisin, (who was ballet director and principal dancer.)

As Le Voisin and Le Raincy were both pupils of the same professer, and were throughly versed in his compositions, they had no difficulty in concerting a scena from a ballet, known by both, which, to the Terpsichorean corps, should have the appearance (when executed) of an improvisation, but to the public, should seem an essential portion of the piece, It was necessary that the conductor of the orchestra should be privy to the arrangement, that he might prepare what related to his department and give the cue.

As for rehearsing, both lady and gentleman declared it unnecessary; or if either of them, (as Le Voisin observed,) in absence of memory, should rely on imagina-tion, it must be forgiven; perhaps, indeed, improvisation would surpass the prescribed effect.

But the manager did not like trusting to chance; so to prevent all mistakes, it was agreed they should meet that evening in the library of his house, in Golden-square; the conductor of the orchestra with his violin and the music-score; the autocrat to preside, sole audience. He would, he said, have the carpet and tables removed, and every thing in order.

To such shifts and contrivances, in the early career of the ballet, was the manager driven by the dread of unruly and rebellious subjects, fully aware that they could not be replaced that side the English channel; and bent, therefore, on every occa-sion on showing their importance, and preserving the monopoly.

Saturday, then as now, was the favourite night, and when any novelty was promised, there was sure to be a crowded audience. The *debut* of a new *danseuse* was actively promulgated in the influential quarters, but without resorting to the channel of the press; a bright star (as the manager whispered) was beaming on the Terpsichorean horizon, which would fill the treasury and entrance the eyes of all; so there came to witness the first appearance of Le Raincy the most fashion-ble and crowded audience of the season. Their majesties were present, in private, with a small suite. Chandos, Burlington, and other nobles, patronising the opera and ballet, or fostering the growing musical taste of the nation, occupied boxes. Handel sat with his Grace of Chandos; and around the circling tiers, interspersed amid the rich array of beauty and fashion, were observable many other luminaries of the fine arts and literature.

After the drop closed on the opera of Rinaldo, the curtain drew up, displaying the opening scene of the ballet, which, as rehearsed, was of trite and ordinary character. The scene was laid in Sicily. A deserter flying from the camp, returns to his native village, and falling in love with a rustic maiden is successful in engaging her affections. On the very day of the marriage-fete, amid hilarity and rejoicing, his regiment marches into the village. He is recognised,' torn from the arms of his bride, summarily tried, and condemned to be shot. The commandant is obdurate, and will listen neither to the prayers of the villagers, nor tears of the bride, who is carried off fainting. His poor distracted father, himself a veteran soldier, presuming on the merit of long and severe services, flies to the cantonment of the general to solicit his son's pardon.

Meanwhile the clemency of the commandant is sought after a mode which affords the usual incident and materiel of a ballet. He is besieged by a group of maidens—the pale and exhausted bride is led to his feet, in vain—nor do the entreaties of the elders of the village meet more favourable consideration. An attempt is then made to dance him out of his stern resolve. with perhaps as much propriety as the captured leader of an army (in the opera) essays to sing down relentless foes. The colonel, however, it is presumed, has the discipline of the regiment too much at heart to listen to such eloquence, and the deserter is bade prepare to die.

The insignificant role (in regard to dramatic interest) of the culprit's sister was assigned to Mademoiselle Le Raincy ; not, indeed, without murmurs from several ladies of inferior station in the corps, but as their complaints were not seconded by those of higher grade. the manager gained his point.

Even in this humble portraiture, where it was imagined there could be no possible display of excellence, Constance evinced superiority, and elicited applause. A precision of step and motion, a seeming absence of effort, drew down many a plaudit, and prepared the spirits of the debutante for higher flights.

The denouement of the ballet, as rehearsed, is consummated by the arrival of the father with the pardon, when all other means had failed, and hope was despairing ; and the natural ebullition of the villagers' joy finds expression in a graceful dance, in which the deserter, (Le Voisin,) and his bride, take the lead.

But in the representation, as concerted by the complotters, a scene is interpolated from another ballet of a somewhat similar character, though more vigorously drawn, the production of the late professor.

Before the father returns, when the distress is at its height, the sister (Le Raincy) approaches the commandant with a slow, mournful step ; she kneels, is rudely repulsed, and a villager, indignant at the treatment rushes to her aid, and is about to lift her from the ground and bear her away.

It is at this juncture that the interpolation commences. The leader of the orchestra gives the signal by a flourish, up starts Constance, with a single bound, which places her far beyond reach of officious aid, a few steps, rapid and flashing, places her again in front of the truly embarrassed commandant.

This took the house by surprise ; not the incident, but the celerity of the movement, and applause rang round the circle ; but ere the audience had time to give expression to the first burst of delight, their senses were rapt by the rapid motions of the danseuse subsiding instantaneously into the statuesque repose of a humble supplicant. The roof re-echoed the plaudits.

The confused and bewildered colonel acted his part to admiration, for his embarassment was real—whichever way he turned, Constance was at his feet, there was no escape.

At a loss what to do, he attempted to retire, and leave the stage to the bewitched maiden, but this she would not permit. By aid of signs, and pointing to the cottage where her brother is confined, she makes known her wish to be admitted. He assents, or rather the inquiring glance which he casts behind the scenes to take cue from the manager, or leader of the ballet, she accepts as acquiescence, and in a tumult of joy yields herself to a wild. delirious dance.

The deserter, (Le Voisin, of course *au fait* to the scene,) who was guarded in the cottage, rushes forward to contemplate the delirium of his sister. She beholds him, and regains her composure—sobbing, she hangs over his neck, and tries, in vain, to remove the manacles. To the many turns of joy, sorrow, and rapture, her measured steps as she walks slowly round the prisoner, and again as she leans her head on his shoulder, the orchestra lent the happiest aid. To prevent betrayal, the musicians were only furnished, after conclusion of the opera, with a score for the occasion, provided by the conductor.

As his sister, with subdued grief and reluctant resignation, is hovering over her brother, the father returns with a pardon. This is the signal for the bride and the villagers—as in the rehearsed ballet—to rush upon the stage. The happy father leads the betrothed to the bridegroom's arms, whilst the sister clasping her hands on beholding her brother's happiness, displays the tumult of her delight in a brilliant luxuriance and abandon of motion—the triumph of the night—which elicits loud resounding applause, and the most exuberant enthusiasm of the audience.

The bride (represented by the principal *danseuse*, vexed and mortified beyon endurance) rather dragged by, than accompanying Le Voisin, executes the finale and the curtain drops.

Constance was handed in triumph by the manager to his sanctuary, where she found the Benningtons, who had witnessed her *debut*, and were waiting to receive her. Overwhelmed with congratulations and compliments; oppressed by conflicting sensations, she begged to retire. With as much pride, and perhaps more pleasure, as his interests were so deeply concerned, as though he were really escorting her Grace of Portland, the flattering autocrat ushered our *danseuse* to her coach. The beaux and idlers, hastily forsaking the boxes, ran behind the scenes, and to the green-room, to catch a glimpse of the enchantress. The vestibule was lined with admirers, who followed her to the carriage steps, cheering her departure amidst the waving of a forest of hats.

Deep joy in many of its moods is akin to sorrow. Constance was unable to support conversation with her delighted friends, and under the plea of excessive fatigue, excused herself from joining the supper-table, where a select party of the Benningtons' acquaintance were assembled in honour of the occasion.

She sought shelter in her chamber. Her heart was full; her proudest hopes realized; the fondest and most enthusiastic anticipations of her late master verified. But where was he who should have shared her triumph? Who had watched through many a year the growth of her budding talents; cheering the pupil through a long course of toil and discipline; kindling enthusiasm by expatiating on the future glory of a bright, prosperous career; where was he now? And her mother—the kind parent, unvarying in her affections? In the tomb—both!

CHAPTER VII.

THE path was now smooth, both for manager and debutante. Her rivals felt so completely out-manœuvred that opposition was entirely vanquished. A general resignation, if the late principal *danseuse* were displaced from leading *roles*, was indeed threatened, but the manager unhesitatingly declared that Le Raincy and Le Voisin alone, would carry him through the season, and that he could, without regret, dispense with the services of the others. This bold manifesto had the desired effect; murmuring was effectually silenced.

As the station and prospects of mademoiselle were now determined, her style o living and expenditure became matters of consideration. It was resolved she should continue to occupy her present location. An elderly lady, a distant relative of Mrs. Bennington, was engaged as companion to accompany the *danseuse* to and from the theatre. In addition, a tire-woman—and that indispensable luxury to one in the situation of Constance—an equipage, constituted her establishment.

Annoyances, which Mrs. Bennington prophesied, and from which the manager had undertaken to protect her, made Constance feel that her path was not strewn with roses. She was beset and pestered with the attentions and gallantries of many of the fashionable rakes, beaux and titled profligates, both old and young, who infested the opera. It was not wholly in the manager's power to shield her effectually from the annoyance ; many individuals, of the above-named classes, were influential patrons of the house, personages of distinction, whom it behoved him not openly to offend. Guarded by native modesty and reserve, confining attendance at the opera to the hours of rehearsal and performance, she evaded the impertinent addresses of some, and the importunate flattery of others. But there are men— and the reign of George the Second was least of all free from such pests—whom no refusal silences, no rebuke deters. Such was the Earl of Headington.

The peerage-book proclaimed his age fifty-three ; his appearance more than confirmed it—he might have passed for an older man. A gloating simper lurking round the mouth and eyes, dwelt in lieu of the open smiles of youth, or the serenity of a matured manhood. A form slightly bent, so slightly that whilst the earl was talking to one of humbler station it might have been construed into an attitude of condescension. Such was the untiring suitor of Constance, who became her shadow, following her behind the scenes, waiting on her to the coach-door, even occupying a seat at the chapel she frequented. Seeking her everywhere, and everywhere repulsed, he at length laid siege to the good lady in Tavistock-street.

One afternoon, after the busy portion of the day, when few or no customers were likely to be met with, the earl ventured into the milliner's show-rooms. Mrs. Bennington was at dinner, A gentleman-customer was not an unusual phenomenon, and his lordship's entry excited no particular surprise. After casting a hurried glance at the wares, and a more deliberate gaze at the showy-looking damsels, he requested to see Mrs. Bennington.

" 'Tis too bad," exclaimed the lady, when she heard the summons, "I thought every one knew my dinner hour. A gentleman, too!—an elderly gentleman. Do you know his name ?"

The girl who carried the message replied, that the gentleman would neither give his card or announce his name, but—

"But what ?" exclaimed Mrs. Bennington hastily.

" I'll tell you his name," replied the assistant, " as we go down stairs."

On the landing the girl said she was sure it was that old, wicked Earl of Headington. He was often in the habit of annoying her and the other assistants when they walked out, and indeed, he was well known all over London as a bad old fellow.

Mrs. Bennington readily imagined what the earl wanted, as Constance had complained of the annoyance from his persecuting attentions. On waiting on the gentleman he requested to be shown the newest and most costly fashions, as he was anxious to make a choice and acceptable present. After selecting, and paying for the articles, Mrs. Bennington requested to know where they should be sent.

" They have not far to travel," replied the earl, with a condescending smile, "if Mademoiselle Le Raincy, as I am informed, lives in this house."

The lady suppressed her indignation with difficulty. Was mademoiselle, she asked, aware of the gentleman's intentions ?

"My dear Mrs. Bennington," said the other, "you must surely know that a gift is prized tenfold by being unexpected."

" Miss Le Raincy is now at home," said the milliner, calmly, " I will announce her good fortune."

The earl attempted to recall her, but the lady was too nimble; she affected not to hear, and closed the door.

When Constance heard from her friend what had happened, she burst into tears, and begged her protection. See him she could not, nor would not.

"I do not ask, nor wish it," said the milliner, "nor was it my intention you should see him. I am a match for twenty such as he."

Mrs. Bennington, on returning below, said the gentleman had committed som mistake, as the present could not be received, and that being the case, she shoul be happy to return the money.

"There is no mistake, my dear lady," said the earl impressively, "there is no mistake beyond the natural diffidence of a young girl."

"And you think," rejoined the milliner, "it would be becoming in Miss Le Raincy to receive presents from a stranger?"

"We will be strangers no longer, madam," rejoined the earl with a simper, "I am Lord Headington."

"Then I hope his lordship will understand me," exclaimed the lady, very emphatically and significantly, "when I declare that there is no course left open for him but to receive back the money."

"That is candid," said the earl, looking keenly at the lady; "I perceive I am misunderstood, and I deserve it for the over-sight I have been guilty of. In the hurry of making these purchases for mademoiselle I forgot that I had with me a present for another lady. May I beg your acceptance of this trifle, and pardon me for neglecting to hand it before?"

As he spoke he handed Mrs. Bennington a morocco jewel-case. The milliner may perhaps stand excused, being so much accustomed to receive money from customers, that her hand was instinctively stretched forth to receive the case, but was as quickly withdrawn.

"Nay, it will not bite!" cried the earl, laughing.

Opening the case himself, he displayed to view a diamond-necklace; the stones were very large. Taking a paper from the interior, he asked her to do him a favour to read the contents. To this request Mrs. Benington made no objection. It was a bill of sale and receipt from a fashionable jeweller, for one thousand guineas, the cost of the necklace.

Lord Headington watched the eyes of the milliner with eagerness.

"My lord, I am sorry to say," cried the milliner, returning the bill, "that my taste is so homely I am obliged to follow the example of my young, diffident friend, in declining your magnificent present. Perhaps your lordship will not take it ill that I leave you to find your own way through the shop."

The latter remark was occasioned by her observing the perplexity and vexation of the earl. His confusion was so great that she thought he would be glad to be left alone. Longer parley might bring on an unpleasant scene. He was a nobleman, she sagely reflected, of powerful and widely-spread family connections; to make an enemy of such a man were detrimental to her business. A calm and civil course might induce him to give up hope, and beat a quiet retreat, which were far better than provoking him *a l'outrance*.

Mrs. Bennington did not, till long afterward, acquaint Constance with the earl's proffer of the diamonds; but she advised her to pursue the same behaviour she had observed hitherto, of sedulously avoiding his lordship; and she trusted that the reception he had that day met with, would cause him to abandon his unworthy designs.

Meanwhile Constance received other attentions far more flattering. Queen Caroline, a lady of wit, spirit and judgment, a patroness alike of philosophy and the gay arts which embellish life, and to whom her consort, the second George, was much indebted for judicious counsel and advice, was, as we have before mentioned, a customer of Mrs. Bennington. On occasion of calling at the show-rooms, she commanded that, at her next visit, Mademoiselle Le Raincy should be present;

her majesty being desirous of seeing whether the young debutante were as amiable in private as she appeared on the stage.

When the queen again visited Tavistock-street, Constance, in acquiescence with the royal will, was in the ware-rooms. After several turns, making some purchases, and more inquiries, her majesty addressed the *danseuse*, asking many questions respecting the artists, musical and Terpsichorean, of the *Academie Royale*. Her subjects, she declared, were much happier than their sovereign ; they could visit, at pleasure, every capital of Europe, while she was condemned to stay at home.

"And I revenge myself as I best may," added the queen, smiling, "for I have stolen Handel from all Europe, and hope I shall be rich enough to bribe Mademoiselle Le Raincy to stay with us."

"I am proud to say I am your majesty's own subject," replied the blushing maiden.

"And France cannot, then, really tempt you ?"

"I would willingly, if it please your majesty, live and die in England," rejoined Constance.

"Then assuredly," exclaimed the royal personage, "we will not hesitate to declare war on account of so loyal a subject."

Here terminated the interview. Her majesty was accompanied to the carriage-door by Mrs. Bennington, leaving Constance to ponder on the last words of royalty, which conveyed a significance beyond what met the ear. On the milliner's return, she beheld her young friend occupying the same spot on which she answered the questions of the illustrious visitor, and absorbed in deep reverie.

"Will you take gold for your thoughts, Constance ?" asked Mrs. Bennington, with a smile.

The danseuse, startled from her brown study, distressed and frighted by half-formed visions of peril, which swept across the eye of imagination, requested explanation of the queen's parting remark.

"How can you expect royalty to talk like humble folk ?" asked the lady with a glance of quiet archness. "Ministers of state, you know, speak in riddles and parables, which will bear any meaning they choose ; and her majesty has caught the tone by listening to it so often."

"And a certain lady, I suspect," observed Constance, "has caught the tone from attending the wives and daughters of ministers of state ; but she who talks in riddles can best expound then."

"Then come up stairs and listen to my exposition."

Our heroine was informed that the news of her success, as might be expected, flew quickly across the channel, conveying to her uncle, and the management of the Academie Royale, the secret of her refuge. The French court, either instigated by the management, or, (as was more likely, if the whisper were true, that Louis had cast an amorous eye on the pupil of the Academie, and was on the point of making proposals, when she took flight,) prompted by the monarch, instructed its ambassador at St. James's to support the claim of Monsieur Le Raincy (now in England) to the runaway, inasmuch as she had fled from lawful guardianship, and from a ratified engagement at the opera, for the fulfilment of which, the uncle, on her behalf, stood pledged in bonds to a heavy amount.

The British king laughed heartily at the application of his brother of France and referred the claim to the privy-council, jocosely recommending them, if possible to avoid war, as the laurels he had won at Dettingen might wither in combating a potentate so chivalric and erratic as Louis. The queen, who had, on several occasions, witnessed the performance of Constance, was much struck with her beauty, and as much pleased with her modest and graceful demeanour. In the belief that Mlle. Le Raincy was a subject of France, and that his majesty's council would, perchance, favour the claims of her uncle and guardian to the custody of his ward, the queen felt inclined to interfere. Our danseuse, as her majesty surmised, might have fled to escape the libidinous designs of Louis—from domestic tyranny, or, perhaps, to elude fulfilment of a treacherous compact between the kinsman and the monarch; but, lest the shield of royal protection should be flung over an un-worthy object, the illustrious lady determined on previous inquiry. From Mrs. Bennington was gathered a concise history of the young maiden; the cruel usage she had undergone in France, and the uncle's unnatural behaviour; with the gratifying fact, (suppressed in Monsieur Le Raincy's claim,) that she was a native-born subject of England.

Mrs Bennington ventured to express to the royal ear the distress which Mlle. Le Raincy would experience on hearing that her kinsman was in England; and hoped that, if the law could not be interpreted in our heroine's favour, that the power of the throne would be exerted to prevent the maiden's surrender. Her majesty condescended to quiet the fears of the good lady, by assuring her, that as it appeared Constance was a subject of Great Britain—a fact as yet unknown to the privy-council—the Frenchman's appeal would be forthwith dismissed. "Though, had it proved otherwise," to use the queen's words, "we would have been loth to have parted with her to so bad a protector; and we can appreciate the ballet as highly as our neighbours."

It was at this interview that the queen commanded the presence of the young fugitive at the next royal visit to Tavistock-street, adding, that Mrs. Bennington had better refrain from making known to our heroine the proximity of her unwor-thy kinsman till it was in her power to communicate that his suit was definitively dismissed. Suggestion from such a quarter was, of course, a law to the milliner. which accounts for the ignorance of Constance, as to the real object of the queen's visit, and the silence preserved by Mrs. Bennington. Le Raincy's claim being finally disposed of, which her majesty very graciously communicated to the milli-ner, the seal of secrecy might be safely broken to the ear of the danseuse, when accompanied with an antidote to the alarm which his powerfully supported preten-sions would otherwise create.

"He is then in London, and I never knew it," exclaimed Constance, after listening to Mrs. Bennington's narrative.

"You look as pale as though you were in Paris, and in his power," said her friend, laughing. "Why, bless me!" she added, "you are actually trembling! Now this is ridiculous. Remember there is no Conciergerie in the Haymarket. Have you no faith in me, no confidence even in the queen's own words, are you not an English woman; what's the use of *habeas corpus* or magna charta if you tremble so?"

Though unable to bear testimony to the merits of *habeas corpus*, or construe other legal phraseology, which chance threw into the speech of Mrs. Bennington, the understanding of Constance was convinced, through the kind greetings of royalty, that her uncle had no control over her actions or liberty; yet, spite of reflection, the force of early. uneffaced associations, lent a terror to his name and person which reason could not wholly subdue.

CHAPTER VIII.

Though Le Raincy was foiled in his attempt to recover the guardianship of Constance, he resolved, ere he quitted England, to try the effect of an appeal to the feelings of his niece. For this purpose, he asked an interview. The request, conveyed through Mrs. Bennington, when announced to our heroine, threw her into a tremor which but too plainly showed how deep was the impression of his tyranny. If she had followed the bent of her feelings she would have declined the meeting, but pride forbade that she should give cause for the opinion that she dare not face her uncle. Mrs. Bennington also coincided in the propriety of granting the music-seller's request. Constance, however, stipulated that her friend should be present ; and though he much disliked the condition, Le Raincy was driven to the acceptance of any chance, however desperate, which promised to forward his views.

At the meeting, which took place in Tavistock-street, he wisely surrendered all pretension to custody or guardianship. She was of age, he admitted, to form her own plans and make her own engagements ; but if she reflected, she could not but acknowledge that her present notoriety and station were owing to his happy

CONSTANCE AND LA VOISIN IN THE BALLET.

selection of her profession. But whilst sunning herself in the smiles of fortune he trusted that she would not forget that her present prosperity was attained at a very serious cost to himself. He was bound, she was aware, under a heavy penalty, on nonfulfilment of the conditions, that she should appear on the boards of the Academie Royal. The time fixed for her appearance was long passed—he was prosecuted in the courts for recovery of the penalty—the only grace he could obtain was an order from the king to stay legal proceedings till he had had time to proceed to England to recover his niece. For himself, continued the uncle,

No. 5.

after being an eye-witness of her triumphs in the Haymarket, he was prepared to abandon the pretensions he once claimed; but he could not suppose that she would suffer him to fall a victim to the suit of the Academie.

This was an adroit appeal to the feelings of a generous nature, and made an impression. Even Mrs. Bennington—to whom our heroine turned for advice—with all her shrewd worldliness, could not gainsay the probability that affairs stood with Le Raincy as he represented them, and that he might suffer a considerable loss from the law-suit.

But her conscience was clear that she was in no way indebted to her uncle, and that in flying from his illiberal protection, she violated no obligation either to him or the Academie—and a single effort of memory sufficed to cast off the meshes of his sophistry, whilst it recalled the indignation which she felt when—in imaginary triumph at having outwitted a defenceless kinswoman—he produced the record of his engagement on her behalf with the Directory. With memory of the affront was restored the glow of defiance which it kindled. Regardless of certain preparatory argumentative attempts of Mrs. Bennington to vanquish the music-seller's position, Constance, in a few brief sentences, reminded her kinsman of his former unworthy practices against the happiness of her mother and herself—and that with respect to the suit of the Academie, she had only commenced a prosperous career—if it deserved to be called prosperous—but notwithstanding his ill conduct to her, should he be cast in damages, she would defray the amount.

Although our heroine's promise extended to all that was claimed by the music-seller, yet he had his own reasons for being much dissatisfied with it, and proposed, that in lieu of her engagement to provide for the damages awarded to the Academie, that she should compound by a present payment. One more experienced than our heroine might have suspected, from this offer, that Le Raincy was already tolerably well assured against loss, and that whatever sum he extracted from his niece would be pure gain; but although Constance did not entertain this shrewd suspicion, yet her singleness of purpose proved a shield as effectual as the most subtle worldly knowledge. 'Twas sufficing to her, as a rule of conduct, that she had made up her mind as to what she ought to do on the occasion; and proposals for a different course, without proof that what she contemplated doing was repugnant to justice, were therefore entirely inoperative. Having been induced, partly by a feeling of pity, partly by generous impulse, to take upon herself the burthen (should it prove so) of the Academie's suit, she could not comprehend why he should—after having gained what he strove for—propose to accept a sum which did not amount to above half the penalty, unless it were through the instigation of his wretched avaricious temperament, which prompted him to grasp an immediate partial benefit, in lieu of more distant, though complete protection from threatened evil.

Her generosity would not permit her to take, what she deemed, an unfair advantage of his infirmity—it was in vain, therefore, that he offered to relinquish all claim in consideration of an immediate payment. She had, she declared, contrary to her intentions before the meeting, now made up her mind to bear the whole brunt of the suit, and an agent in Paris should be properly instructed both to watch over the legal proceedings and to liquidate the award.

Finding, at length, that he could not change her resolution, he quitted his niece, disconcerted, out of temper, and uttering ill-deserved remarks on the ingratitude of people towards those through whom their own fortunes have been made.

Mrs. Bennington was vexed with our heroine, that she should be so deluded (as she called it) by the artful music-seller, as to promise to shield him from the consequences of the villainous engagement he had contracted, but the lady's husband, when he heard the particulars, laughed heartily at the good generalship of Constance, who had (unconsciously it must be admitted) out-manœuvred and foiled her uncle with his own weapons. It was palpable, he said, that Le Raincy had received an indemnity against the law-suit before he quitted Paris, and it was more than probable that he pocketed a handsome fee in consideration of his embassy. His pretensions were supported by the French ambassador, and his negotiation no doubt originated with the ambassador's master. It was quite consistent with the general tenor of the agent's conduct that he should endeavour to obtain a second indemnity, but the cool style in which he was defeated by mademoiselle was really beyond all praise.

Meanwhile the season was drawing to a close, and as if fortune meant to recompense Constance for the anxiety she had suffered from the presence, in London, of the intriguing avaricious kinsman, her other persecutor, the notorious Headington, appeared to have given up his unworthy importunities. He was still in town, and as usual a close frequenter of the opera, but his pursuit of our heroine slackened, and his assiduities in another quarter countenanced the idea that he had abandoned an impracticable suit for an easy conquest.

Amid all her triumphs, Constance had not forgotten the home of her childhood. She visited the house, and by permission of the tenant explored each well-known room and garden-path. Together with what was treasured in memory, rushed other long-forgotten scenes. As she peered o'er the fence of the adjoining garden, she was, in imagination, again a child. But where was Arthur Edmonstone—where her dear parent? Of what avail the loud plaudits of the opera, the nightly triumph, to the forlorn sickened heart? Tears sprung to her eyes as she walked alone in the garden, recalling "to the sessions of sweet silent thought" remembrance of the past.

Mr. Edmonstone, she learned, was dead—a stranger occupied the house—the residence of Arthur was unknown, though it was believed that he was alive, and in London or its vicinity. Would he not recognise a name so popular, or at least, notorious? was the question she oft asked herself, as she rode homeward from Kensington. And if he did recognise it, would he not visit her? Alas! if he were prompted by remembrance of the romantic friendship of their childhood to renew it at a maturer age—she had been long enough in London—yet he came not! Had years made him proud, worldly, or selfishly indifferent?

But Arthur, to whose history we must now return, deserved not these reproaches. His father established him as a merchant in the city; the subsequent decease of his parent, to whom he was sole heir, added to his wealth and extended his influence. Both before and after his father's death, he occupied a house in Austin-Friars above the business offices. The dwelling in Kensington which the old gentleman occupied on lease, was surrendered to the owner, as the young merchant, after the fashion of those days, deemed it reputable and prudent to reside at the place of business.

But though he quitted Kensington, its memory was deeply endeared to him. His father peremptorily forbade the correspondence which Arthur, with boyish enthusiasm, undertook to commence with Constance when she left Kensington for France. He was now his own master—years had passed away—he had become a man, and was enthralled by the inevitable anxieties of commercial affairs. But he turned with delight from the speculations of commerce and the attractions of society, to that sunny period, which memory preserved unbroken, when Constance was his playmate and friend.

The fame of Le Raincy spread—the name startled him—he was led to visit the opera. In the dark lustrous glance, and elegant contour of our heroine, he could not identify the modest playmate of childhood, but certain passages extant in the history of the danseuse, which were the subject of familiar talk in the gay world, convinced the young merchant that she was the same. He would have introduced himself, but the eager impulse was checked when he heard of the titled host of admirers which surrounded her, and of the hauteur with which she treated them. How much was she misrepresented! The reserve interposed as a shield against the importunities of such men as the Earl of Headington was magnified by rumour into a disdainful pride, so elated with success, as to look down with scorn on the homage of the great and gallant. "What chance—when nobles were repulsed—had a merchant with such a temper?" He was conscious also of the misconstruction which might not unfairly be placed on the motives of one who had neglected the friend of his childhood when she was of private, if not obscure station, and attempted to renew the intimacy as soon as he beheld her environed by the blaze of prosperity.

But though withheld by these considerations, from seeking her society, he became an ardent worshipper of the new divinity, was invariably present on the evenings she appeared, and shared in the triumph, whose notes he helped to swell. A gay acquaintance, in a former season, had in vain persuaded Arthur to stroll with him behind the scenes of the opera, where he had the privilege of introducing him, both at rehearsal and during performance; but it was a step deemed by our young merchant so likely to prejudice his reputation in the city, that he declined. Yet he was now eager to avail himself of his friend's experience in exploring a path so beset with lures and temptations.

Having acquired a knowledge of the localities of the labyrinth, and some insight into the characters of those who frequented it, he came alone, that he might indulge the secret pleasure of gazing on Constance, himself unnoticed, unknown. Her beauty suffered no disparagement—as proved the case with others—by near inspection, but admiration was lost in a deeper feeling when he discovered that she was totally without pride or affectation—that she was familiar and affable both with the servants of the theatre and the members of the Terpsichorean corps, and that the scornful hauteur of which she was accused, was only raised as a defence against the libertine and importunate gallant. Her path, though strewn with roses, was planted with thorns. A new experience of life was opened to his view—he saw the nature of the perils to which one in the envied position of Constance was exposed. Was she not rather an object of pity than envy? But whilst trembling for her welfare, he could not contemplate, without enthusiasm, the high spirit of his old playmate which sustained her through snares more obvious even to the spectator than the intended victim.

Often their eyes met. His frame was thrilled, but the glance of Constance was cold and impassive, and was quickly transferred to other objects. Fain would Arthur have broken through his timid restraint and have spoken, but there were ever some personage of quality or importance at her elbow to witness his bashful approach, and mayhap, repulse; the words he had summoned died on his tongue, the momentary courage fled from his heart.

As the scene he entered on was new, so were the characters and personages he encountered. Unknowing and unknown, a spectator merely of the motley throng in which he mixed, he had complete leisure to detect many a subtle manœuvre and scheme, but he had eyes only for Constance. All who approached the object of his secret admiration were subjected to the closest scrutiny; the open practices, therefore, of the Earl of Headington could not escape him. The more he learned of the earl's character, the more he saw of his actions and behaviour, so much the deeper was the contempt he felt towards him. But mingled with contempt for her persecutor was extreme solicitude for Constance, and certain events occurred which redoubled his anxiety.

Arthur, as we have hinted, was not unconscious how much endangered was the stability of his reputation as a merchant of rising character and influence, by constant attendance behind the scenes; and during his moments of self-communion, he strongly battled the point that he should at once cease treading such an unequivocal path, or manfully disregard the press of gallants, and approach the lady with what success he may. Whilst debating this point, he by chance overheard a conversation which had the effect of reconciling him to his late and present course, both as regarded his reputation, and to his distant, hovering pursuit of the brilliant star of the Haymarket.

Peril threatened her, secret undermining peril, of which, if successful, she would fall the victim, ere she were aware of the danger. Could he earn a better title to her esteem than by thwarting it? By defeating the machinations against her peace, he became her defender, her champion, even the very office which he ad dreamed of in his boyish day-dreams and romantic reveries!

CHAPTER IX.

MR. EDMONSTONE, who oft remarked with feelings of contempt and indignation the practices of the old earl, following our heroine with fawning, spaniel-like step, from her attiring-room to the stage, from the stage to her attiring-room, was much astonished to behold his lordship's assiduous attentions transferred to another object, by whom, we may observe, they were received with very evident complacency. But Arthur was not so pleased with the change as Constance, who was too much delighted to be freed from her tormentor to speculate on the cause. Taking into consideration the old man's character, the desertion was too sudden and abrupt to be ascribed to despair or disgust. Whilst our young merchant was seeking a clue to the mystery, there came behind the scenes, one evening, a stranger. He soon singled out Lord Headington, and drew him apart. The visitor was a man about forty, of compact, martial figure. Gold lace (rather tarnished) on the coat, and a cockade in the hat, bespoke the military profession. The features were heavy and impassive, the complexion sallow ; his cheeks, which were marked by a deep furrow downwards to the corners of the mouth hung folded over the cravat. But the eye contradicted the general expression of his physiognomy —it was bright, active, and restless, and continually wandered from the party addressing or addressed. Altogether, the appearance of his lordship's acquaintance was far from being calculated to win confidence ; it was just such an aspect as would throw the merchant or banker instinctively on his guard, as against a man of guile or pretence.

Whilst Edmonstone was scanning very closely the new comer, he heard his name pronounced from behind, and on turning, beheld his friend, Harry Neville, to whom he was indebted for his passport to the green-room and adjacent regions. Mr. Neville proposed adjourning to a neighbouring coffee-house to sup—to which Arthur was averse, though he did not positively decline.

"Come, come, Arthur," said the other, taking his arm and dragging him away, "I have a little advice to give. These boards are like what the boys call cat's-ice —they may, perhaps be skipped over in safety, but to stand gaping, as I caught you, one is sure to sink seas over in ridicule—a confirmed laughing stock."

When seated at supper, Neville renewed the subject.

"Whose eyes have shot the shaft, Arthur, which transfixed you so thoroughly?"

"There is but one whose sway I would own, throughout the wide domain of opera-land," replied Edmonstone, "and she, if you please, shall be our toast."

"Well!" observed Neville, gravely, "the earl has declared off, sickened, and taken a new fever ; there is hope ; but the man who wins her must not stand like a basilisk ; a statue won't charm her, I'll swear—but here's to the fair Le Raincy, and the success of Austin-Friars against all St. James' and the Haymarket."

Conversation continued in the same strain during the supper, after which Arthur's gay friend proposed taking him to a club in the neighbourhood, but the other refused, and they parted for the night. Returning homeward, Edmonstone passed the stage-entrance of the opera-house ; the door was open ; he had, in fact, managed to leave his friend earlier than the latter wished, in expectation that he should have another glimpse, ere he retired to rest, of Constance, whose performance in the ballet would detain her till a late hour. As he entered the badly-lit passage, or corridor, he heard the voice of Headington, who was approaching. To avoid being recognized—for the young merchant was in truth ashamed of his second visit, at that late hour, to a place so noted for intrigue and dissipation, although he did not suspect that the earl knew his name or profession—he turned aside, in the deep gloom, under a staircase.

Headington passed, accompanied by the stranger. They paused at the door, in deep conversation, which was carried on in a low, earnest tone of voice,

Edmonstone could neither retreat nor advance without being discovered; indeed, he did not expect to escape unseen, and instinctively felt for his sword (it was the fashion of the day to wear one), as he suspected that the man with the tarnished lace (if not his titled friend), might accuse him of eaves-dropping, and prove a quarrelsome customer. As they did not pass into the street, and relieve him from his disagreeable position, Arthur stood debating, whether he ought not to step forward and attempt an explanation, which the delay of every moment rendered less likely of being candidly construed. The dialogue was carried on in so low a tone as to be scarcely audible to the at first unwilling listener. Many sentences were uttered of which he did not catch a single word, but from others he gathered enough to learn that some plot was in agitation, having reference to Constance, and that Headington's companion was preparing to put it in execution.

"No! no!" uttered the earl, with a complacent chuckle, " not till the season is over, all St. James' would start in pursuit of the hussey were she missed now."

The indignation of Arthur was so strongly roused by the remark, that he was only restrained from chastising on the instant the pair of unprincipled plotters, by reflecting, that such a course would in nowise serve Constance, and that he should draw on himself a quarrel without having detected the nature of their machinations; whereas it was most essential to the safety of mademoiselle, that the design should be known, in order to guard against it. He was, however, disappointed of further revelations, for a carriage drove up, the steps were lowered, and the two worthies were carried off, to discuss, unheard, their nefarious design. Arthur's mind was at once made up to the course he should persue—to watch unseen over the safety of Constance, and endeavour to unravel the plot, but failing this latter aim, to defer no longer than the close of the season introducing himself to Le Raincy, and putting her friends on their guard.

Constance found the season flitting without hearing from or seeing the companion of her childhood. Amid the loneliness of life, and the persecutions she endured—for the Benningtons' time was much occupied with their own affairs, and they could not, either with propriety or convenience, attend her everywhere—to recover a lost friend (she hoped a trusty one), would be indeed to find a treasure. And much need had Constance of friends. Little knew she the villany long meditated and now matured.

The last night of the season was appointed for her benefit. It proved a golden harvest in regard to profit, and displayed the extent of her reputation. Garlands and wreaths were showered at her feet. The queen sent a handsome necklace of brilliants in the morning, which she wore during the performance of the ballet.

The Haymarket was so crowded with carriages that Constance, to avoid the delay of waiting, after the performance, for her equipage to approach the door, ordered the coachman to stay in an adjoining street, intending to find the way to it on foot. But on being escorted to the vestibule by the manager, she was agreeably disappointed by a servant in her livery, and whom in the hurry she supposed was her footman, saying, that her carriage now stopped the way, and that the constables were ordering the coachman to drive on. The door was immediately opened, and Constance hastily bidding the manager adieu, stepped in, and the vehicle rapidly drove off to make room for others.

The Benningtons, who could not deny themselves the pleasure of being present at their friend's benefit, finding that Constance did not come to their box, after the performance, as usual, threaded their way in safety through the crowd to the appointed spot, where was waiting mademoiselle's carriage, and in which was seated the lady who officiated as companion to our heroine. In reply to Mrs. Bennington's surprise at not finding Constance, the lady observed that she had waited in the green-room mademoiselle's return from the stage, but to avoid, as she was informed, the press of compliments which awaited her, she made a hasty retreat by the manager's aid to her carriage.

Mr. Bennington, much surprised, returned to the theatre and inquired for the manager. He had gone home, but had been seen handing Mlle. Le Raincy, into her coach.

"It must have been his own carriage," muttered Bennington as he returned, "she has, perhaps, found herself unable to resist an invitation to supper in Golden-square."

After explaining how matters stood, he proposed that they should return home, and send the carriage to Golden-square with mademoiselle's companion as escort. Mrs. Bennington, whose fears were more active, would not listen to the arrangement, but decided that they should stop in Golden-square in the way home. Her spouse dissented; as it might wear the appearance of a wish to be invited—but he was overruled, and they drove thither accordingly.

The surprise of the manager was extreme when he learned that it was not her own coach into which he handed the *danseuse*. On their part the Benningtons were as much surprised to find that their friend's disappearance could not be explained by the manager. Both parties concurred in the suspicion of foul play. But what had the footman to say for himself, asked the manager; if he were at his post, he should have been at the stage-door waiting to attend his mistress?

But the footman had been ordered, in accordance with prior arrangements, to remain with the carriage, as Constance intended to avail herself of Mr. Bennington's escort.

"An arrangement which I helped to frustrate," remarked the manager.

"Mademoiselle, on hearing that many of her admirers were waiting in the house to offer their congratulations, was in a hurry to escape. Perceiving her distress—'tis strange she should fly from homage proffered so devoutly—I offered my services to lead her to her coach. In the eagerness to escape, she must have forgotten her engagements with you—but I trust all will yet be well."

The manager, however, did not leave the restoration of Constance to chance. After promising the Benningtons to call early next morning, he hurried off—though it was a very late hour and he had invited several friends to supper—to the Haymarket, to recover, if possible, some clue to the abduction. He was in truth—though he passed off the matter rather lightly—much alarmed. The imposture of an equipage—in livery and appointments a fac-simile of our heroine's—was proof of a carefully matured plot, and bespoke ample means to carry into execution the base designs of the originator.

The manager's arrival was eagerly looked for in Tavistock-street. But he brought unwelcome news—he had no tidings to tell of Constance, nor had he gleaned any information which might either indicate the whereabouts of her retreat, or point suspicion against any individual. He did not feel justified in making Miss Le Raincy's mysterious absence public, by application to a magistrate, or employing the aid of the police, till he had received the sanction of the Benningtons.

Whilst debating on the most expedient steps to be taken, the card of Mr. Arthur Edmonstone was handed to Mrs. Bennington with a verbal request of an interview.

"Arthur Edmonstone," said the lady, glancing at the card, "I do not know the name."

"Nor I," cried her spouse; "what can he want?"

The servant replied that he was a tall young gentleman—rather confused in his manner—he desired to see one of the family—but would prefer seeing Mrs. Bennington.

"I admire his taste," observed the manager smiling, "but I have a suspicion that this gentleman's visit is in some way connected with our friend's disappearance, and with permission, I should like to remain in the house till after his departure."

"You shall be present, sir, unless he wishes otherwise," replied the milliner. She requested the gentleman to be shown up stairs.

Mr. Edmonstone, after seating himself, glanced round the room, and then addressing Mrs. Bennington, wished to be informed whether he was correct in his belief, that Mademoiselle Le Raincy formed one of the family.

Mrs. Bennington and the manager exchanged glances. The milliner replied, that he was certainly correct in his belief, but she understood from her servant that he asked to see Mrs. Bennington.

Arthur replied that such was the fact—still he was disappointed at being deprived of the pleasure of seeing mademoiselle. In fact, he came to see both ladies—he had formerly the happiness of being known to Mlle. Le Raincy, and should be much gratified in renewing the intimacy—and he had also a circumstance of importance to communicate regarding mademoiselle, which he would prefer imparting, in the first instance, to Mrs. Bennington rather than to the young lady.

This announcement was sufficiently mysterious to arouse the curiosity of all present. The good lady was puzzled. Constance, of course, could not be produced; neither could the cause be assigned to a stranger, why she was not forthcoming. She said to Edmonstone, that he must be aware madenoiselle had very arduous professional duties to perform—that her habits, in consequence, could not accord with the ordinary family-routine—last evening was her benefit night—she hoped, therefore, that he would not take it ill, or as a breach of courtesy, if the introduction were deferred to another visit, which need not, however, delay the communication to herself.

Mrs. Bennington and her visitor retired to a distant window-seat, out of hearing of the two gentlemen. They had not conversed many minutes, ere the lady started up in agitation and running towards the manager, exclaimed, " the mystery is cleared—that villanous old earl is at the bottom of this roguery."

Mr. Edmonstone, in surprise, followed, begging the lady to be composed, and speak in a lower key, or the affair might reach the ears of mademoiselle without due preparation.

"Constance has gone, sir," retorted Mrs. Bennington, wildly, " she was carried off last night—your warning comes too late."

Arthur stood aghast, confounded with the startling abruptness of the lady's manner, and the calamity which it announced.

" I see it is my turn now," said the manager, stepping forward; " Mr. Edmonstone, I was not aware of your name till this morning, but I have seen your face behind the scenes, and you will no doubt recognize me as the manager of the opera, and of course deeply interested in everything which befalls Mlle. Le Raincy. The warning which our friend, Mrs. Bennington, just now spoke of, you will perhaps see no impropriety in communicating to me."

Arthur said he would only withhold it one moment, till the suspense which he suffered respecting the fate of mademoiselle was relieved.

After mutual explanations, Edmonstone was taken into council, to devise the most fitting and expedient mode of procedure to recover our lost heroine. To tax the earl openly were deemed unwise, as he would of course deny the charge as a base calumny—no proof, of any weight, could be advanced—neither would such a course help to detect where Constance was held in durance, and from the skill and address exhibited in accomplishing the abduction, it was a fair inference that similar cunning would be displayed in the selection of a hiding place.

CHAPTER X.

Ere the conclave separated, Mrs. Bennington received a note, without a signature the writer of which sneeringly thanked her, in broken English, for the protection she had afforded mademoiselle Le Raincy during her stay in England.

"What think you of this?" asked the lady after reading the contents.

"That it might have occasioned us some perplexity," replied the manager, "if Mr. Edmonstone had not fixed so clearly the stigma on my honourable and noble constituent. The trick is cunning, yet by no means sagacious, for if Mr. Le Raincy of Paris had carried off our Helen, he would not have been the fool to expose himself to detection by writing this scrawl, before even he had time to clear the kingdom. No! 'tis a mere device to divert our search into a wrong quarter."

APPLICATION TO THE KING IN COUNCIL TO RETURN CONSTANCE TO PARIS.

"Besides," observed Mr. Bennington, "I had occasion to ascertain that Le Raincy quitted London several weeks ago."

As the Earl of Headington was a leading supporter of the opera, and possessed, from rank and connection, considerable influence with other subscribers, it was decided that the manager should be relieved from the task of encountering the noble profligate, although he was both from duty and inclination, prepared to make any sacrifice on behalf of our heroine. Arthur was the chosen chivalrous knight. Unlike Mr. Bennington and the manager, his business could not possibly

No. 6.

suffer detriment from the anger or malice of the earl, and the zeal already displayed in the affair gave ample promise that he would prove an efficient champion.

After Edmonstone quitted Tavistock-street, on his way to the dwelling of Lord Headington, and not before, he began to reflect seriously on what he had undertaken. It scarcely admitted of doubt, that his lordship was concerned in the abduction of Constance; yet on what ground tax him with the crime? It was known to all London (the gay portion of it) that the earl was an admirer of the danseuse; that his importunities were pressing, and had been incessant. Yet that was no evidence on which to build a charge of abduction; neither would it prove to Arthur a very valid argument of defence should his lordship prosecute him for calumny. Yet what step, short of making a distinct charge, was available in gaining a clue to the present abode of Constance? To tell his lordship that Mademoiselle Le Raincy had disappeared under very mysterious circumstances, and, thereupon, ask him if he were a party to the act, were puerile, and, at the same time, an insult which no gentleman could brook.

" And why were not these points discussed in Tavistock-street?" muttered Arthur in soliloquy; " the fact is, these two very sagacious gentlemen have permitted my hot-headed zeal to carry me where I can neither advance nor retreat. If I managed my affairs in Austin Friars as clumsily, I should lose all credit on 'change."

The dilemma appeared so grave, that Edmonstone was on the point of giving up his visit till he had arranged some more feasible mode of proceeding than either taxing a gentleman with a crime without other proof than a conversation overheard only by himself; or, on the other hand, asking him for a purely gratuitous confession of his guilt. Why, in the latter case, supposing the party innocent— and he will, of course, assume all the indignation of innocence—I should be kicked down stairs as an audacious calumniator!

The predicament in which Arthur, in imagination, placed himself, forced a laugh, spite of the seriousness of his position. But, as he was on the point of turning his steps homeward, the image of Constance crossed his mind. Is this proud voluptuary to break, at will, through every restraint, and know no law but force? No no!—come what will, I'll beard the brute in his own den; and these pleasant gentlemen, my good friends of Tavistock-street, who pitted me to the encounter, shall never know that I shrank from the temerity of it!

As these reflections passed through his mind, the pride of the young man was kindled, and every prudential consideration gave way before it. It was about noon when he knocked at the door of the earl's mansion, in Hanover-square. Arthur handed his card, and, after a short delay, was ushered through a library into a retired study, where sat his lordship in a well-cushioned library chair, enwrapped in a dressing-gown, with feet in slippers resting on a stool. The breakfast equipage stood within reach. At the moment of Arthur's entry he was sipping chocolate with an air of languor, and in an attitude of confirmed feebleness, in striking contrast to his reputation as a gallant

Edmonstone had prepared himself to receive an intimation that the earl had quitted town, or was indisposed. The facility with which he was admitted rather staggered, for a moment, his conviction of his lordship's agency in the carrying off Le Raincy, till he reflected, that were he denied to visitors, or had left London, it would afford just ground for suspicion.

As his lordship pointed to a seat, the expression of his face hovered between an habitual simper and curiosity to know his visitor's business. Arthur, in fact, was in no hurry to commence—he was pondering on the storm which would so soon succeed the present complacency.

" From the city, sir, I perceive," uttered his lordship, glancing at the card.

Mr. Edmonstone bowed assent.

" We cannot do without you gentlemen of the city," continued Headington with an inquiring look, "we are forced sometimes to pay you a visit—but—my man of business has not informed me of any contemplated arrangement."

"Your lordship mistakes," replied Edmonstone, who perceived that his backwardness in announcing his errand was leading the earl into an error, "though I come from the city, my visit has no reference to business. It is with your lordship as a patron and supporter of the opera that I have to address you."

"Hah!" exclaimed the nobleman, with more vivacity than he had yet displayed.

"My troubling your lordship is in consequence of the disappearance of Mlle. Le Raincy. There is no doubt that she is the victim of some vile plot. She was handed into a carriage, which she believed her own, and there all traces ceases."

Headington stared at the speaker with real or affected astonishment. After a pause, he asked—

"Have you been round to all the subscribers, Mr. Edmonstone with this announcement?"

"No, my lord," replied the young merchant, who affected not to be sensible of the sneer, "I began with your lordship, as the leading subsciber, and as a warm patron of the talents of mademoiselle."

"May I inquire, sir, by whom you were employed?"

"I came by request of her friends in Tavistock-street. It was presumed that the calamity which has befallen the lady would very much interest the frequenters of the opera, and that they would make common cause with her immediate connections, in unmasking the villainy which has been practised against her, and aid their efforts to discover whither she has been carried."

"Hah!" murmured the earl, relaxing into his previous languor, "Mademoiselle Le Raincy—why I saw her only last night—it was the night of her benefit."

"She never reached home, my lord; she entered a carraige which in appearance so resembled her own, that she could not possibly entertain suspicion."

"It was a cruel act," observed Headington, leisurely, "but I know not, sir, how I can aid you,"

"Your lordship was a constant attendant at the opera, and had every opportunity of observing Mademoiselle Le Raincy, and all who approached her. Carrying your memory over the last season, do the actions of any one who came in contact with the young lady strike you as being suspicious—such, in fact, as might lead to the inference that he was the author or the agent of the vile conspiracy of which she has fallen a victim?"

"Mr. Edmonstone," said the earl, with rising displeasure, "I believe you forget yourself; I am unused to be spoken to with such freedom; yet I can pardon the act in consideration of the feelings which dictated it. I know not to whom you allude, or whom I could suspect, even if I dare. I am much concerned at the success of the stratagem which has been practised on Le Raincy, and I sympathize with the feelings of her friends on the occasion."

"I am glad to hear your lordship so express yourself," said Arthur, with earnestness, "it gives me a confidence, which I should not otherwise have possessed, to utter what I have to unfold."

The earl elevated his eyebrows, in quiet surprise, at the pertinacity of the visitor, who would not depart, and leave him to quaff his chocolate in peace.

"I have my suspicions, my lord, which—"

"Sir!" exclaimed Headington, looking at his watch.

"I believe, my lord, I know the author of the villainy we so much deplore."

The earl attempted to rise, but Mr. Edmonstone prayed him to be seated a minute longer. Looking the elderly voluptuary full in the face, he narrated how, a few evenings since, he overheard, at the stage-door, a conversation, which he repeated, word for word.

Headington made several attempts to rise, and was deterred by the earnest gestures and language of Edmonstone.

" Can your lordsihp now hazard a guess at the identity of the party ?" asked the merchant, when he had concluded his narrative.

"Your audience has lasted long enough," replied the earl, gaining his feet and moving toward the bell-rope.

" Stay, my lord," cried Arthur, placing himself before the nobleman, " it was the earl of Headington whom I overheard plotting with a vagabond-accomplice."

" Eh ? eh ? will you offer violence to an unarmed man ?"

" Not unless your lordship attempts to fight by proxy—but call for help, or make the least noise, before I have said what I have to say, and asked what I have to ask, and even the consideration of your age shall not prevent me puttting my foot upon you."

This speech was uttered in such a tone of vehement indignation that the earl feared to provoke the threat which it embodied. He stood passively waiting what might follow.

Believing that he had made an impression on the fears of the voluptuary, Arthur lowered his tone, and proposed, on behalf of the friends of Constance, that if his lordship would name the place to which she was carried, or restore her to her home, that the affair should terminate without exposure.

Headington made no reply.

The merchant reiterated his proposal, adding that he was in himself evidence of the earl's agency in the abduction—that the author of the villainy being known, the forced retreat of the young lady could not long remain undiscovered—and that no expense nor pains should be spared to bring to justice the actors in the disgraceful affair. It was in the power of Lord Headington to prevent these unpleasant consequences, simply by surrendering Mlle. Le Raincy, or disclosing where she was concealed—and he awaited a reply.

Still the earl was silent.

"May I know your lordship's final resolution ?" asked Edmonstone.

" I have already told you, sir, that I am unarmed—I have so far yielded to your threat, that I have raised no alarm—you are free to stay, by your own lawless will as long as you choose—but the sooner you depart the better for my comfort, and perchance your own convenience."

And so saying, his lordship dropped again into his easy chair, and commenced sipping his chocolate. Arthur was provoked almost beyond endurance by this coolness—his frame heaved with passion.

" Would to heaven," exclaimed the merchant, looking sternly at the old profligate, "that you were a younger man—I must go, lest I be tempted to lay hands on you. The pillory may be your portion yet."

A momentary stare was the only reply—but his lordship's hand shook, and the beverage was spilled on his knees.

" You spurn my offers," uttered Arthur, "but rest assured that justice can, and shall reach the high as well as the lowly—agent and aecomplice, both—both shall meet their deserts."

Thereupon the indignant merchant turned on his heel, and quitted the house.

"He's too old to drub—he's too feeble to measure swords," soliloquized Athur as he walked toward Tavistock-street, " yet I'll spend twenty thousand rather than he shall escape ! My poor Constance, what misery are you now suffering after such brilliant triumphs !"

The manager had agreed to wait Mr. Edmonstone's return from Hanover Square. He listened with extreme interest to a recital of the interview.

"There was no alternative," he observed, " but to make a direct charge—yet no one but you, Mr. Edmonstone, who overheard his infamous plans, could, with propriety, in the present stage of the business, tax him with his conduct. But what can we do next ?"

There was an extreme aversion to make the affair public, by laying the case be fore a magistrate, lest the reputation of Constance should suffer. So many varied rumours of the story would get afloat, which the friends of the earl would propagate to injure her character, that an application, except as an ultimate resort was deemed both unwise and unpalatable. Yet the longer Constance remained undiscovered, the more peril she risked, the more distress she endured. It was finally agreed that the remainder of the day should be spent by the manager and Mr. Bennington in the prosecution of inquiries in and about the Haymarket, and that the parties should meet again at night in Tavistock-street, when a final course of action should be arranged.

CHAPTER XI.

During the walk homeward, Edmonstone, after revolving a variety of expedients, was quite at a loss what course to pursue with regard to Lord Headington, who appeared to set equally at nought the chances of exposure and the strong arm of the law, but he no sooner beheld the face of Francis, the house-porter and valet, a shrewd knowing fellow of about fifty years of age, than he began to entertain fresh hope and spirits.

Francis was formerly valet to a major-general, a dissolute voluptuary like Headington. He had oft diverted his present master with anecdotes of the adveutures, scrapes, and intrigues which he had witnessed during his former service. He had a wide connexion, much more so than was relished by the merchant, with grooms, valets and others of the like class at the west end, with whom he had been in habits of intimacy whilst in the service of the general. Francis was too often absent at the fashionable quarter of London, reviving old reminiscences, when he should have been in the staid, quiet precincts of Austin Friars; but to counterbalance these delinquencies he possessed many excellent qualifications which Arthur would have found it difficult to replace.

With the prompt decision, learned in the conduct of mercantile affairs, he resolved to make a confidant of this man. Francis, after being enjoined to secresy, was told every particular relative both to the abduction of Constance and the proceedings of the Earl of Headington, nor was withheld from him the motives which prevented her friends from applying for legal aid. Could he possibly ferret out the lodging or place where mademoiselle was detained?

Francis, after a few moment's consideration, replied with a smile, that Mr. Edmonstone might indulge some hope of his success, he knew the way to Lord Headington's servants' hall, but he should want money. With means at command, and reasonable good luck, he trusted to make a report by to-morrow morning at breakfast, but he wished it understood, that he must not be expected to name the parties from whom he gained his intelligence. What he might perchance reveal must be taken on his own credit, without corroboration from other authority, nor must Mr. Edmonstone divulge, even to the friends of mademoiselle, the source whence he gleamed his intelligence.

This stipulation was deemed by his master reasonable, more so, perhaps, than the amount of money, he asked for twenty guineas, but he declared on his honour that he entertained no expectation that any portion of the sum would remain in his own purse.

When Arthur visited Tavistock-street, in the evening, he found Mrs. Bennington utterly disconsolate, there was no tidings of her young friend, nor any clue by which she could be traced. An appeal to a magistrate appeared the only course, but Arthur's report gave encouragement, and it was agreed that the strong arm of he law should not be yet evoked. At breakfast, next morning punctual to t e engagement, Francis presented himself. The substance of his information was to the effect that the confidential valet of his lordship was away from the mansion bound on some enterprise of importance, and that his master was secretly preparing to follow, though ostensibly making no preparation to quit town. It was the opinion of Francis, no doubt based on other facts in addition to those communicated, that Mlle. Le Raincy had been carried into the country, that every precaution was taken to prevent her forced retreat being discovered, or to implicate the earl in the abduction. According to his own assertions, Francis had no doubt of being able, in the course of one or more days, to trace the lady to her abode, but more money would be required, as well as patience, and it was highly probable, he added, that the personal services of Mr. Edmonstone would be required in completing the search.

Arthur, whose mind was strongly inflamed with two incentives to action, the desire to recover Constance and to thwart and punish the earl, promised the man five hundred guineas for himself if they succeeded in rescuing her without resort to the civil force, and in the meantime whatever sums he might require to prosecute the inquiry.

In observance of Francis' stipulation, Mr. Edmonstone informed his coadjutors that he must withhold from them the name and condition of the agent through whom he was working; but it remained for them to declare whether they were content to wait the development of the inquiries he had commenced, or resort to other measures. The policy of appealing to the law was again discussed, but they all concurred that such a course might be the means of attaching a slur to the reputation of Constance, not easily to be removed. That the earl, as other gallants had done in similar instances, would boast that the lady was not an unwilling prisoner, and that he was not the less happy that his good fortune was made public. Whereas, were she privately rescued from his grasp, the chance of scandal would be avoided. Arthur was therefore entreated by the gentlemen, and beseeched by the lady, to continue the pursuit.

But it is time we returned to Constance. As the carriage drove off, she found herself alone, and began to upbraid herself for her precipitancy in running away without her companion and the Benningtons. She pulled the check-string, intending to give orders to the coachman to return to the spot where she had arranged the coach should wait for them, but the string was loose. It was a negligence the coachman had never been guilty of—she tapped against the pannel, but the noise was unheeded, owing, as she imagined, to the unusual rapidity of the vehicle. The blinds were thrown up, which in the hurry she had not noticed— she could neither lower them nor open the door. The side and front windows were also blocked up. On making this discovery she grew alarmed, suspecting treachery. If she could but break, or remove the blinds the glass would offer but a slight obstacle to her crying for assistance, but all her efforts were in vain! She found herself in a moving prison, traversing the streets at a rapid pace, passing perchance many a noble heart and courageous hand, which would eagerly have flown to her rescue; but alas! she was unseen, and her cries, if at all heard, were heard but for a moment. She became aware that the coach was purposely planned to prevent all chance of escape or rescue. And what was to be the denouement of a villain who employed such foresight and preparation? She trembled at the thought.

Meanwhile, the paved streets were left behind, and the coach rolled over the smooth suburban road. The momentary, flashing gleams of light which had hitherto penetrated her dark prison, became few and far between. The carriage stopped—she could distinctly hear that the horses were changing. Now was the time to make herself heard and bring rescue! She renewed her cries and repeated the blows. Footsteps approached the door, and a voice besought her to cease. Frantic with joy, she awaited her deliverance. Alas! the cruel disappointment. She was briefly given to understand that no aid was near; not a soul but the servants of the equipage—that they were on a lone heath—that the spot was purposely chosen for the relay, that she might have no chance of rescue.

—and if she doubted the speaker's word, the door should be opened. The offer was declined—Constance shrunk from the idea of encountering the gaze of the ruffians. She was then informed that no violence was intended ; that the end of the journey would be more pleasant than the commencement, but that attempt to escape, or raise an alarm by her cries, was useless. The unhappy lady made no reply, but sunk on the seat in deep dejection.

Many hours passed, during which she remained in a stupor of grief, from which she was only roused by a partial dissipation of the obscurity. The grey light of dawn twinkled through the crevices of the blinds, but the interstices were not sufficiently wide to afford any glimpse of the road over which she was travelling. Of a sudden the coach stopped—the door was opened, and discovered the hall and staircase of a dwelling-house. She was asked to alight, and she was but too glad to quit the coach, though it should prove, alas! but a change of prison. The vehicle was purposely drawn close to the wall, that she might not see the exterior of the house or the surrounding country, to identify either on any future occasion. But in descending, her eye caught a passing glimpse of the ocean.

There is a torpid state of mind which does not prevent the perception of impending danger, or even speculation on the means of escape from it, but paralyses the will. Constance beheld herself the victim of conspiracy planned with skill, which it would require all her energies and courage to elude, yet in descending from the coach she uttered no cry, nor did she make appeal to the fears or sympathies of those who surrounded her. In the hall she met a woman of middle age, who announced herself the housekeeper, with orders to wait on the newly arrived guest. Our heroine inquired to whom the house belonged. To the captain, was the reply, but the name of the captain, the housekeeper could not, or would not, divulge.

Was he at home? demanded Constance with anxiety.

The woman replied that he came from London by the same vehicle which brought mademoiselle, and that he would doubtless enter the hall in a few minutes, as breakfast was prepared according to orders sent down yesterday. Perceiving Constance agitated, she invited her up stairs, to the apartment arranged for her use.

"Must I go up stairs," asked the young lady, looking wistfully around.

The housekeeper made answer, that, in the parlour, breakfast was prepared for the captain, and in the room on the other side of the hall—which comprised the only chambers below furnished, except the kitchen and offices—the captain's people would take breakfast, and she imagined mademoiselle would prefer to sit alone.

Constance made no reply, but followed the woman up stairs.

She was ushered into a parlour, or sitting-room, fitted up with care and elegance. The breakfast-table was adorned with rare china and silver-plate, and laden with delicacies which, at a happier season, after a long journey, would have been delightful. Adjoining was a chamber, where, said the housekeeper, mademoiselle would find a toilet and change of raiment ; in fact, everything needful.

On entering, Constance perceived that the windows were barricaded, cross-wise, with thick oaken bars. This told a tale which needed no comment. Returning to the parlour, she discoverd that the windows were protected in the same fashion.

The housekeeper invited her to commence breakfast.

Hunger and thirst are imperious, though the mind be ill at ease. She sat down, and the other poured out a cup of tea. Constance, however, declined tasting it till her attendant drank of the same beverage. The woman, who previously was affable and attentive, looked angry and disconcerted, and demurred to the request.

"You told me but now," said our heroine, gravely—and looking her full in the face—"that you had orders to obey me in everything."

The housekeeper assented.

"Then drink this tea, as I tell you, or you may fare badly for disobeying orders."

This was an argument which the other understood. She immediately drank the tea. Constance had entertained a suspicion that it might be drugged, but after waiting a few minutes, and observing that the woman suffered no ill effects from it, and reflecting, moreover, that it was of her making, she commenced herself.

The long, forced night-journey, the mental distress, and constrained posture of so many hours, after brilliant and fatiguing exertions on the boards of the opera, had thrown her into a state of weariness and despair, from which she now gradually revived. With reanimated spirits and courage she plied the house-keeper with questions, none of which were answered, unless they happened to be of a trivial character. Finding she could not coax information, she attempted bribes—at least the offer of bribes, for she had only promises to offer—but the attendant was proof against them. Her master, she said, was richer than made-moiselle, and could outbid her. The rejection of her offers made our heroine angry. She lost temper, and threatened the woman with the terrors of the law, which would assuredly overtake every accomplice in the wicked conspiracy. The other answered sullenly, that she would be faithful to those who employed her, and on their shoulders must rest the responsibility.

She was thereupon ordered out of the room, and told not to return till sum-moned by the bell. Taking away the breakfast equipage, the woman departed.

Our heroine immediately went to the door—tried it—it was fastened on the outside. She entered the chamber, the outer-door of which was also firmly fastened. The windows opened, but the bars prevented egress. Opposite, at a distance of only half-a-dozen feet, or thereabouts, a thick shrubbery, of lofty growth, shut out the view of road, meadow, or lawn, or whatever lay in that direction. She had certainly caught a glimpse of the ocean, and she fancied when she listened, that she could hear its hoarse murmur. It must be the sea-coast of Sussex, Kent, or Hampshire, she could not tell which, for the woman was artful, and thoroughly on her guard, and would not admit even that they were near the ocean.

But Constance did not despair. The Bennington's were firm friends, and would not rest till she was restored to them. The queen was a kind patroness. The manager was not devoid of sincerity. Regard for his credit would force him to join her friends in their search. She had a suspicion that the earl was the author of the villainy, but her belief did not amount to entire conviction, as she had seen him lavishing much attention on another lady. But her doubts, she be-lieved, would soon be set at rest, for about an hour after breakfast, the house-keeper returned to say that "the captain," desired an interview. Was the "cap-tain," only another name for the Earl of Headington?

It was not the earl. There entered, with an air of extreme deference, the same individual whom we described seeking his lordship behind the scenes. Constance fancied that the face was not unknown to her, yet she could not recollect where she had seen it. He commenced by expressing much concern for her health, and hoped that the unavoidable roughness which she encountered on the journey would now be atoned for. The house, and all that was in it, was at her disposal, and he was himself her most humble servant to command.

"Will you conduct me to the nearest inn or village?" asked Constance, after listening till he ended his protestations.

He should be happy—but it was totally out of his power.

"Then you will not prevent my finding the path myself?" cried Le Raincy, seizing her cloak and bonnet, and moving towards the door.

"Pardon me, mademoiselle," replied the captain, placing himself against the closed door, "I ought to have mentioned that, although everything within the house is at your service, you must not—cannot quit it—night and day, till I am relieved from my post, you are watched and could not if you wished, escape."

"Bear witness," cried Le Raincy, indignantly turning to the housekeeper, "that this man detains me here by force. In a court of justice you shall testify to this."

"Why, mademoiselle, you would not, surely, think of leaving the house in that dress!" uttered the woman.

Constance glanced at a mirror. She was in the costume in which she took leave of the audience, but the apparel was disordered, her coiffure was disarranged, her face pale and haggard. Casting on the floor the cloak and bonnet which she brought from the theatre—her entire wardrobe—she burst into tears.

YOUNG EDMONSTONE'S INTERVIEW WITH THE EARL OF HEADINGTON.

The captain muttered a few words, expressive of his intention to renew his visit when she was more composed, and quitted the room. The housekeeper endeavoured to console the poor lady by describing the changes of apparel and dresses, which were in the wardrobe, at her command; but Constance, during her brief career, had imbibed a touch of the fiery impatience which characterises the spoiled children of fortune, and she cut short the woman's eloquence by an order to leave the apartment. As the door closed, Constance detected that it was fastened by a spring on the outside.

No. 7.

CHAPTER XII.

THE history of Captain Henderson, though not uneventful, varied but slightly from the career of many of his gay contemporaries. He was born to a good estate, and came into possession of it ere he arrived at that age in which experience generally corrects the errors of youth. At college, his expences exceeded his guardian's very liberal provision; he ran into debt with several Hebrew money-lenders, who grow rich by supplying collegians with the means of riot and extravagance. When he became his own master he discharged the usurers' demands, and, having already dipped deeply into his inheritance, readily listened to the a guments of those who pleaded that he might just as well, for a season, taste the delights scattered in his path, though it were at the expense of a few thousands more, and then—to use the well-known phrase—having known what life is, he could reform, retrench, and, by frugality, restore his dilapidated fortune. So also argued Henderson himself, prompted by evil passions and dissolute associates, equally treacherous. If he could have kept away from the gaming-table, his career might, possibly, have stopped short of ruin. His intellect was sound and acute, and a liberal fortune is not quickly wasted by a possessor who exacts an equivalent for all the gold he parts with. Our young adventurer was free from most of those foolish weaknesses which would have permitted others to make his purse their own. This was soon perceived, and, as his companions were of that class which hang around a child of fortune for sake of spoil, they found it necessary to extract that by fraud, which they failed of obtaining by mere cajolery. Even his better qualities were adroitly trained to his ruin. In games of mingled chance and skill, an astute intellect finds some scope for exercise and delight. He was taught to feel the excitement of play, and was glad to escape from mere dull sensual gratification to a pursuit in which he discerned zest and enjoyment. He lost deeply, and in seeking to recover his losses, was irretrievably ruined. Perceiving the way affairs were progressing, he bought a military commission that he might not become wholly destitute. When ruin was complete—when he had nothing more to lose, he joined the herd by whom he had been plucked, and became himself one of the creatures which prey on society. In this condition, the captain, of course, lost character and caste, and his intercourse, thenceforth, with people of quality, was of rather an equivocal character. Though his income was straitened, habits of luxury were deeply rooted, and to supply pressing exigencies, he was not above becoming panderer to the vitiated tastes of Lord Headington—from such a degradation there could be no lower fall.

The lone manor-house, on the sea-coast, was yet, nominally, his own, though heavily mortgaged. Its situation, remote from town, hamlet, or neighbours, made it peculiarly desirable for the earl's purposes. It proved the best card the captain had played for many a day. He was liberally supplied with money to furnish the house anew, and pay the overdue interest on the mortgage. A woman, whom he had some knowledge of, the widow of a bankrupt-tradesman, was installed as house-keeper. The under-servants were also selected by the captain, who took care to engage none on whom he could not rely. In fact, the entire preparation for, and plan of the abduction of Constance was entrusted to the management of Henderson, and its success proved the extent of his skill and capacity for such villanous schemes. The activity of the agent was of two-fold service to the principal. It enabled the peer to afford undivided attention to his parliamentary duties, which, toward the close of the session, pressed heavily on members of the house, and also permitted him the opportunity of remaining in London, after the disappearance of the danseuse, immersed in his usual pursuits, and thus give the lie, practically, to any charge that might attach to him.

Though Henderson had not contemplated any ulterior purpose when he first offered his services to Lord Headington, to aid him in his villany, yet it was impossible for a man of his sagacity and selfishness to avoid entertaining speculations with regard to his own interest, both prospective and contingent, arising from the adventure in which he was embarked. It was not alone sensual passion, but vanity, which prompted the earl, and he was prepared to pay dearly for its gratification. For sake of the eclat of having Constance under his protection, the withered beau was prepared to run into any expense or extravagance, and contemplated with serenity, the ultimatum of a very handsome settlement.

Henderson had no room for complaint on the score of inefficieet reward for services, yet his imagination was forcibly struck with the idea that he might reap imdortant advantages by studying his own interest without regard to the wishes of his patron. Would not a marriage with Constance prove far more conducive to his welfare, than permitting her to fall a victim to the practices of the old beau? Her ample, nay, splendid professional income must, in time, clear off the mortgage, and her good conduct and modest demeanour secure the countenance and acquaintance of those parties whose esteem was most desirable, whilst her husband would be restored to what he deemed his proper station in society.

Nor were the means by which he sought to realize his ambitious views inadequate. He had custody of the fair prisoner. If he remained faithful to his unholy compact she must fall; but if he thwarted the earl, he won a claim to her gratitude, which she could not more gloriously repay than by a union with himself. Nay, he held the cards so firmly, that he could make marriage the sole condition of his interference. Take heart and courage, then, brave captain! What an ignoble stake, in comparison, had he played when flinging on the board his rouleaus of gold!

Yet the game required deep skill, foresight, and above all, control of temper. Unlike the earl's scheme, force would not win the victory. It was essential to penetrate the character of Le Raincy; he must even study those who surrounded her; for he needed both associates and dupes. The housekeeper, Mrs. Harris, was engaged by himself, and might therefore, in some measure, be considered in his interest. Yet, in tutoring her how to behave, it was necessary to make her acquainted with the history of Constance, and the intentions of his lordship, and he perceived, with alarm, how much her vanity was gratified on finding herself in a position to be of service to so powerful and wealthy a nobleman. In fact, she was much delighted with the idea of his visit, and with the familiar and confidential part she was to play in the affairs of the peer.

Such being the case, it was necessary to proceed with caution. If he failed in bringing Mrs. Harris over to his views, he ran imminent risk of being ruined. Would she keep secret his proposals, was the anxious question, or would she not, rather, if she declined them, strengthen her influence with his lordship by revealing the treachery of his agent?

Henderson, as yet, had had no private conversation with her since his return from the metropolis. As soon, therefore, as she was so unceremoniously ordered from the presence of Constance, she was summoned to the captain's parlour. Mrs. Harris, in her youth, had been accounted pretty, and had received the usual attentions which the other sex pay to beauty. After marriage, a series of vicissitudes impaired her personal charms. The neglect of her husband, and the absence of admirers, fretted her vanity. Accustomed to be petted and caressed, she could not endure neglect; her temper was soured, her spirits broken. She grew envious withal, and hated those whose youth and gracefulness attracted the admiration which she could no longer claim. This trait had not escaped the keen observation of Henderson; he recognised the spiteful glance and insidious speech, and detected the lurking, disappointed vanity to which they owed origin. Such a woman, he was certain, would entertain but little sympathy for the unfortunate Constance. who owed all her peril to her charms. She was, therefore, a fitting instrument, and poverty made her a willing one. As she entered the captain's apartment, her countenance betrayed the ill-temper which stood gathered on the brow, elicited by the peremptory behaviour of the danseuse.

"Slt down, Mrs. Harris," cried Henderson, in his most affable manne

The housekeeper, with an ill-concealed anger, excused herself on the plea that she had much to attend to—that her presence was required among the servants.

"Stay, stay," cried the captain, "I have also much to speak about. How fares it with our prisoner!"

"What, yonder tinselled wench!" uttered Mrs. Harris, scornfully. "I thought his lordship admired nature, not paint."

"You are too severe, Mrs. Harris. It is not every one whose complexion will stand the test yours has experienced. Ten years ago your step was somewhat lighter, but the white and red roses in your cheek bloom as though they would never fade. Charity, however, would better become you than such scorn—you can afford to be generous."

"And this is the French girl whom all London is mad about !" exclaimed the housekeeper, without replying to the captain's compliment, "why what a fuss is made after a passably-shaped light-o'-heel ! A better form and finer features might be met with in London every day, without one-tenth of all this preparation and expense."

"That's very true," replied the captain, gravely smiling, "if Mrs. Harris had been Madame Le Raincy or Senora Picarina, why her worthy spouse would have lost her long before he gave up the ghost."   ,

"Thank you, Captain Henderson, for your opinion of me. To suppose, indeed that any man would have tempted me to run away with him, and forsake my husband—though, indeed, the brute did not deserve much consideration from me."

"Nay, look not so angry at me," observed the gentleman, "I do but speak the truth. The enraptured gallant would have wept, raved, intreated and implored at the feet of the bewitching Senora, and, if she had proved obdurate, would have been carried off by force. A name is everything. I would venture a cool sum, now, that if the earl were not so hot after this Haymarket girl, that if I were only to introduce you to his lordship, as Senora Harrico, he would be enraptured. In contemplation of the serene gracefulness of matured womanhood, he would wonder how his vagrant fancy could ever have been so cheated and ensnared as to run after a lathy, painted French girl."

"Oh! captain—and I am standing to listen to this foolish nonsense !"

And thereupon the housekeeper made pretence to escape ; but she was intercepted.

"But why run away?" cried he, standing between her and the door, " you women will always fly from the truth, yet will stand and listen to falsehood. But you have not told me what passed between you and Le Raincy."

"Nothing worth the telling," remarked the housekeeper, narrating the particulars of what transpired.

"Now what is your candid opinion of the business, Mrs. Harris ?" asked the captain.

"You must speak more to the purpose, sir."

"Well, in plain language, how will she receive the addresses of Lord Headington ?"

"Why, just as she received you and me."

"Ah ! I understand—with indignation and tears, and all that sort of thing—but suppose he presses, what then ?"

"She'll scratch his face."

"And a handsome settlement—a thousand a year perhaps more, will go a begging ?" rejoined the captain. " I cannot believe in such folly."

"That's her temper, trust me. She has a spice of the vixen in her. But what will be done if the girl continue obstinate ?"

"What will be done ?" cried the captain, repeating her words—"Do you imagine that his lordship and myself are to undergo all this labour for nothing? A cutter is on the way here, and she'll be taken on board ; during a sea voyage means will be found to conquer obstinacy. She'll gain nothing by it, and, may be, lose settlement.

" 'Tis a pity this rich lord's money should go a-begging," observed the house-keeper, thoughtfully, " when honest people need it so much."

" So it is, Mrs. Harris," replied the other, " and wise folk would'not fail to take advantage of the golden chance."

" You must speak out plainly, Captain Henderson, if you wish me to list

" So it appears," replied Henderson, laughing.

" Hang this woman," thought the captain, " speak of her complexion and any nonsense will go down; but touch on money matters, and she's as sharp as my old Hebrew friends."

CHAPTER XIII.

HENDERSON was pleased yet embarrassed. The house-keeper was aware that his discourse meant more than met the ear, and had challenged him to speak out plainly. But could he trust her with his confidence? Without her aid, he could scarcely hope to accomplish his views, but should she prove treacherous, he were ruined. In the crooked paths of intrigue and dissimulation, the depraved way-farer, by a fortunate conjuncture of circumstances, is oft enabled to travel to the summation of his wishes without unmasking his designs. But it was not so with Henderson. He needed the agency of Mrs. Harris; and the line of conduct she ought to pursue to serve his purpose was too complicated to admit the possibility of her being artfully driven into it in the character of an unconscious dupe. To gain much, something must be risked. Reason and ponder how he would, there was no escape from this position, so our captain resolved to make a confidant of the housekeeper.

" Sit down, Mrs. Harris," he continued, " there—in that chair by the window— and I'll join you in a second."

He opened the palour-door, took a survey of the hall to make sure that none of the servants were listening, and then seated himself opposite the house-keeper.

" We're old acquaintance, Mrs. Harris."

The woman replied by a significant gesture.

" This is not the first time I have thrown business in your way."

" I am sure, sir, you need not remind me of it—I have never proved un-gratful."

" Have you ever had reason to feel distrust of me—have I ever broken my word, or my engagement ?"

" Never, sir—never."

" Then we thoroughly understand each other, Mrs. Harris."

" O no, sir—I am quite at a loss to guess your meaning."

" Quick—you are too quick, by half—I shall come to business all in good time. Now tell me candidly, what do you expect to gain by this affair ?"

" Why sir, the sum you promised me!" replied Mrs. Harris, with an air of surprise, real or affected.

" True—true. But nothing more ?"

" A few perquisites, perhaps."

" Pshaw! I thought we were old friends, Mrs. Harris. Now I can read your thoughts. You expect to secure his lordship's favour and countenance with a view to future benefits."

" And, I hope, sir—I confess, my wish is to please his lordship."

" And suppose, that by so doing, you reap on some future occasion as much as you will now. There ends your expectancy. Now serve me on this present chance—be staunch to my interests for this once, and you shall earn—not a pal-try sum—but an annuity for the remainder of your life."

"But what do you expect of me—what am I to do, sir, to earn so large a reward?"

"To aid in accomplishing a virtuous act," replied Henderson, with much gravity.

The housekeeper tried to preserve a serene countenance, but failed. She burst into a loud laugh.

"I excuse this on the score of old acquaintanceship," observed the captain, with marked displeasure, "you have known me certainly of old—but I can reform I tust."

"They say, sir, that virtue is its own reward—and I am afraid it might prove so."

"That's sincere!" exclaimed the captain, with the addition of a sonorous oath, which we need not repeat; "'tis true, I am now too poor to grant any one an annuity, but you can help me to fortune if you will, and you shall share my good luck."

He then proceeded to explain, that if the earl succeeded in making Constance his mistress, neither himself nor the housekeeper would be much benefitted thereby; and should he by chance fail, his temper would be soured, and they might both probably lose what they had anticipated. But suppose, on the other hand, that Henderson should himself step in, and thwart the evil designs of his lordship, by marrying Mademoiselle Le Raincy himself. Her large income would build anew his fortunes—the lady must owe a lasting debt of obligation to her deliverers from infamy, and could not begrudge the annuity her husband had engaged to pay one who contributed to such an important service.

Mrs. Harris made no reply for a few seconds, but sat absorbed in deep reflection. She, at length, uttered slowly, as though she were talking to herself, "I shall r in myself with his lordship."

"That's true," cried the captain, "you cannot serve both. You must make your election—you know the terms."

"I am a lone woman, Captain Henderson," uttered the house-keeper, after another pause, "and I depend on my character for a livelihood. If I lose that I lose every thing."

"The d—d hyprocrite!" thought Henderson; "I engaged her precisely because she had no character to lose, and was not over-nice in her regard for such a commodity in others."

"I might lose his lordship's favour," she continued, "without being certain of compensation.

"Why hang it, woman," uttered the captain, in a passion, "I am now prepared to give you a promise, or my bond, in writing, that the annuity shall commence from the date of my marriage with Mademoiselle Le Raincy."

"I agree to the terms," said Mrs. Harris.

The compact was immediately ratified by the captain executing the promised document. The distrust and reserve which hitherto marked the conduct of the houekeeper, gave way to confidence and loquacity. She grew loud in her professions of service, and animated in suggesting modes by which her services would be most available. A glass or more, of wine, exchanged with the writings, lent impulse, maybe, to her zeal.

"I admire now, captain, your cleverness in every part of this business," cried Mrs. Harris, with gratuitous eloquence, "if you had followed the military life as a profession, you must have become a Marlborough or an Eugene. There is but one item which you appear to have overlooked—and you will confess, when I point it out, how strangely blind you have been to your own interest."

"Come let me know it!" cried Henderson, gaily, "how deep is man's obligation to woman's wit!"

"How much do you say his lordship intends settling on the lady, if he succeed in his wishes!"

"A thousand a year, at least—a house furnished, and a handsome equipage."

"And all under bond and seal—no backing out?"

"Every thing as clear and precise as a lawyer can make it," replied Henderson.

"Well, now, Captain Henderson, if I were you—with those heavy mortgages hanging over you, I would prefer taking Miss Le Raincy after she has secured her thousand a year, instead of now, with nothing but what she can get by dancing."

"I take her after!" exclaimed Hederson, rising from his seat in a furious passion; "fire and fury! what do you mean? Whom do you take me for? Here, in my own house—where my ancestors have lived two centuries—to make such a proposal to me? Out of the room instantly, woman—quick—or I may do you some mischief."

His attitude certainly foreboded mischief. In his rage he had seized the decanter, which he brandished aloft after a style which made it very doubtful whether he were practising a rhetorical flourish, or about launching a missile. The housekeeper wi ely sought safety by a precipitate retreat.

"This follows from keeping bad company," said Henderson, after the lapse of a few seconds, in which he had time to cool, "yet there's no help for it—I need the woman's aid after all."

Further reflection convinced him, that to preserve peace, and ensure success, he ought immediately to make overtures of peace, The earl would not stay in London longer than was necessary to establish a fair presumption, by his presence there, that he had no participation in the abduction, or disappearance of Constance. Before he arrived, if no further progress were made, it was essential to the captain's interests that a plan of co-operation should be established between himself and the housekeeper for the double purpose of thwarting the designs of Lord Headington, and predisposing Le Raincy to regard Henderson's approaches, or proposals, with favour.

Mrs. Harris was again summoned to the parlour. She found the captain quite calm and affable. He said, that however well-meant were the remarks which she uttered, that they caused him extreme pain, and he trusted that she would never again broach the subject. Independent of the poverty which led him to covet a wife possessing the means of realizing a large income, he was an ardent admirer of the beauty and modest character of Mademoiselle Le Raincy, and, if a man of fortune, would be happy if she would listen to the same suit which he was now about to prefer.

Mrs. Harris, with many curtsies, said that gentlemen understood their own feelings best, and that zeal for the captain's pecuniary welfare led her to overlook what was due to his station.

Matters were thus amicably arranged, and it was next discussed how they should act towards Constance. Henderson listened attentively to what had passed between the fair prisoner and the housekeeper, and cautioned the latter against losing temper in future interviews. On the contrary, she must bear with her caprices, and endeavour to win her confidence.

"As for myself," continued Henderson, "in the present stage of affairs, she cannot but regard me with hatred and aversion, and I cannot yet hope to make more favourable impression; but allow her, Mrs. Harris, to entertain a belief that you sympathise in her sufferings, and that you would, if you dare, connive at or assist in her escape, and you will establish an influence which will carry us to the haven we desire."

The household functionary, after completing her arrangements in the offices, returned unsummoned to the apartment of Le Raincy. She found her at the open window of the sitting-room, endeavouring, in vain, to take a survey of the exterior. The bars precluded her seeing more than the thick wall of shrubbry in front—she could obtain no idea of the premises, and she withdrew with a sigh, on hearing the approach of her goaler.

The housekeeper, after glancing at the stage-apparel which she still wore, remonstrated with Constance for not availing herself of the abundant change of raiment prepared expressly for her use.

The danseuse emarked sharply, that it was for that reason that she declined using it. Whatever might be the feelings of men, were there no charity, no Christian feelings in her own sex, that one woman could behold another torn from her home and confined like a criminal, without feeling pity for her hapless situation ?

Mrs. Harris, mindful of the cue she had received from Henderson, replied that she did her sex much wrong In supposing that any woman could see unmoved a young lady treated as Miss Le Raincy was treated ; but, alas ! what could a poor servant do ? She was, herself, almost as much a prisoner as Mademoiselle, and was as closely watched, but so far as lay in her power she would gladly exert herself to alleviate the horrors of her harsh situation.

These words were uttered with a crafty semblance of candour, which disarmed suspicion. Indeed, Constance could not believe that any one, except those who had carried her away, could refuse their sympathy. She caught a gleam of hope from these artful expressions, which Mrs. Harris sought to strengthen, by recurring to the subject of Le Raincy's disordered and inappropriate apparel. If mademoiselle scorned to make use of what had been placed at her service, would she refuse to accept a change of a humbler description from the house keeper's own wardrobe ? It was distressing, she declared, to behold a young lady of so much beauty and grace, heart-full of misery, and worn with fatigue and vexation, arrayed in the gaudy finery of a masquerade. Who, in her present guise, would give her credit for being what she really was ?

This was touching the right key. Le Raincy was herself conscious, that should she ever succeed in making her escape, or in regaining her freedom, she would have but little claim on the compassion of those whose protection or hospitality she sought, but in such a guise as she now wore, would be regarded in the dubious light of a strolling-player, or an itinerant dancing girl. She suffered herself, therefore, to be persuaded by the officious housekeeper who readily assisted at her toilet, and by whom she was transformed from the tinselled, yet tawdry and dejected stage nymph, to an appearance which befitted a country maiden of gentility. Our pliant domestic next spoke of dinner, but Constance declared that she was in no humour to sit down to table. Yet Mrs. Harris would listen to no excuse —grief must be fed, she said, eat as heartily as sound health, or the spirits would altogether sink. After dinner Miss Le Raincy might indulge in a few hours repose,—the cruel deprivation of rest rendered sleep necessary—should she refuse to court it, sickness must ensue at a season when she needed all her powers to sustain her through her trials. After sleep, she would awake refreshed, and inspirited, and who could tell but that some happy thought or idea might present itself, which would point the way to freedom

---

CHAPTER XIV.

Our unfortunate prisoner believed that in Mrs. Harris she had found one who sympathized with her troubles, and was not indisposed to aid her in escaping from them. Their confidence grew apace. The housekeeper, in reply to the urgent inquiries of Constance, admitted that exterior fastenings were affixed to the doors of her apartments, and that it would cost her place, if she neglected, in a single instance, drawing the bolts on her prisoner—she added also that all the servants were creatures of Captain Henderson, or rather of his noble employer—that it were utterly hopeless to entertain the idea of making an appea to their feelings. They were selfish, callous time-servers, prepared to excute, without scruple, the behests of those who paid them. Of all concerned in this shameful affair, (continued the artful woman) the only one on whose sense of honour or honesty they could p ce any reliance was Captain Henderson, who had that very morning confessed his bitter regret that he should have become an agent in the abduction of our heroine. But he was poor, overwhelmed with debt—his house he could scarcely call his own —and hence the motive which led him to act the part he had undertaken,

"And you will not deny, then, Mrs. Harris," said Constance, "that his employer is the Earl of Headington?"

The housekeeper reminded her that the question had been thrice repeated, and she felt constrained to repeat the same answer, viz. that several days at most would divulge the name and quality of the party, but that in the meantime, she had sworn not to divulge it. It was only her sense of the solemnity of an oath which withheld her communicating his name; she would however venture the remark, that she admired Miss Le Raincy's judgment and sagacity.

THE FIRST INTERVIEW OF CONSTANCE WITH CAPTAIN HENDERSON.

This was accepted as a virtual confession, and Constance thought she beheld a chance of escape. She very earnestly pressed Mrs. Harris to sound the captain on the subject of permitting her to return home, on the understanding that he should receive a more valuable consideration for his performing an act of humanity, than he contemplated earning by lending himself to a deed of vil'any.

Our wily housekeeper, without crushing the hopes of Constance, replied to the

No. 8.

effect, that if it were not for the necessities which pressed heavily on the captain, she knew he would entirely relinquish his unworthy agency, or rather, he would never have undertaken it, but in the present stage of affairs, whatever were his wishes, he would find it no easy task to escape from thraldom. The earl could at any moment throw him into prison, and although he knew much which affected deeply his lordship's character as a man of honour, yet all that one of his standing could utter against a nobleman of high rank, would be accounted vile calumny. Still there might be ways to move the captain to an act of grace, and any trial were preferable to being subject to the unwelcome visitation of the great enemy of her peace.

The prospect, however vague, of freedom, lent such impulse to the spirits of Constance, that the housekeeper became alarmed lest she had gone beyond the proper line of policy. She broke off the subject, with a promise that all her interest should be employed with Captain Henderson to accomplish her deliverance before the arrival of his employer. To prove that her zeal was not confined to verbal professions, Mrs. Harris furnished Miss Le Raincy with the several keys of the apartments, so that it was in her power, whenever she chose, to lock out intruders. After such proof of the woman's good-will, Constance yielded to her persuasions to sit down to the dinner prepared for her, and at night retired to rest with a feeling of security far beyond what she anticipated.

The captain was overjoyed whilst listening to the report of his colleague's progress, who took especial care to paint in forcible colours the success of her dissimulation. It was agreed, that on the afternoon of the following day, Henderson should pay a visit to his captive, who by that time would, it was deemed, be disposed to regard him with more favour than he met with on his former visit.

After dinner, on the day following, Henderson's wily emissary believing that she had fully prepared the way for the captain, descended to his parlour for the purpose of inviting him up stairs. She was told by one of the servants that he was walking about the lawn or in the gardens. Thither she flew in a great hurry, and found the gallant captain chatting across a low hedge (which divided the flower-garden from the meadows) with a gipsy-girl. The wanderer was wrapped in a cloak and hood, which partially concealed a pair of rogueish, sparkling eyes, and sunburnt features.

Mrs. Harris thought there would be no harm in watching the parties without revealing herself. She stood concealed behind a row of bushes, and listened in silence.

The usual traditionary mode of coaxing the noviciate into a speculative curiosity with regard to his fortune, was not, in the present instance, departed from. If her hand were crossed with a coin, he should see into futurity!

He held out his open hand, from which she took a half-crown.

"You have lately come from a journey," remarked the sybil, after she had pocketed the money.

"I want to know about the future, not the past," said the captain.

"You come from the north," said the girl, peering closely at the lines of his hand.

"Not very far north," remarked Henderson smiling, "or I should not throw my money away."

"You will be exposed to double danger," exclaimed the gipsy, "beware of losing the old friend before you are sure of the new, and I am not sure you will escape from the net spread by one of my own sex."

"Get along with you," cried Henderson, "or you will not escape the constable."

"Stay! stay! captain," shouted Mrs. Harris, coming forward, "do not send her away."

"Oh! of course not," replied Henderson laughing, "if you wish it."

The housekeeper spoke very earnestly for a few seconds with the captain, after which the gipsy was requested to go round to the garden-gate. She was thence led, nothing loth, to the parlour.

Mrs. Harris believed that the gipsey might prove a valuable auxiliary. There are few minds which can resist the influence of a prediction when prognosticated from supposed occult causes, and the housekeeper fancied that if the sybil were instructed how to act, and what to say, that she might cast a spell on the mind of Le Raincy favourable to their plotting.

The girl, as might be expected, had no objection to finger the gold which was offered, nor did she make any objection to act according to the instructions she received. After she had been properly tutored, Mrs. Harris left her to prepare Constance.

The housekeeper commenced by inquiring if she had ever consulted a fortune-teller, or a cunning-woman, and on receiving for reply, that she had never entertained a wish to do so, although she had, on several occasions, personated such a character on the boards, Mrs. Harris remarked that the captain had strolled from home, and finding the coast clear, she had invited into the house an itinerant predicter of future events, known throughout the county for the wonderful accuracy of her predictions. She proposed having her up stairs, to afford a specimen of her art. Even though Miss Le Raincy were above the weakness of putting confidence in the vagrant, still it would help to while away the time.

Constance objected very strongly. She had no spirits, she said, to enable her to sustain the task of talking to strange people, or enduring their prying glances. If her appearance at all corresponded with her feelings, it needed not the skill of a professed sybil to describe, without falling wide of the mark, an anguished heart.

Mrs. Harris replied, that it was precisely on account of the anguish which the young lady was suffering, that she had invited the gipsey to create a diversion by her gossiping nonsense. Besides there existed no source of misery without a means of escape from it, and however dismal the prospects of the present hour, sunshine might illume the path to morrow.

Constance yielded to the woman's arguments—or rather, suffered herself to be persuaded. The red-cloaked sybil was therefore led to the apartment of Le Raincy.

Constance was seated in a capacious arm chair lined with crimson-velvet. Grief had paled her check, and broken her spirits; she reclined in the attitude of an enfeebled invalid.

The gipsey, on entering, gazed intently on the fair sufferer, regardless of the usual forms of ceremonious jargon in which the members of the tribe are adepts.

Constance believing the woman was embarrassed, invited her to take off her hood and cloak and sit down.

"We are very dull here, my good girl," continued Le Raincy, "and I have sent for you to enliven us."

"Do you wish to read your fate, lady?" asked the gipsey, still standing motionless, and eyeing Constance closely.

"O! yes," replied Le Raincy with a careless laugh, "but I'll hear that by and bye—sit down, now,—drink a glass of wine—I should like to hear how such as you live, without house, without a home, exposed to every storm which blows, yet possess more health and content, than those who are better lodged and fed."

The gipsey, emboldened by these words, and moreover by the kindliness of tone with which they were uttered, stepped to the chair in front of Constance. A shower of dark clustering hair fell with careless profusion over her face as she removed her bonnet. An entire absence of any approach to a decent arrangement of the coiffure might be pardoned the vagrant beauty, for the sake of the jetty locks, and the gleaming eyes which peered through them.

Le Raincy remarked as singular, that the gaze of the gipsey was constantly directed either to herself or Mrs. Harris, and that she appeared to eye the latter with suspicion. Even from this trifling circumstance, there sprung a faint hope of the possibility of the gipsey being an emissary of her friends,—a hope which was strengthened by the glance of commiseration or sympathy, which the girl directed (whenever the eyes of Mrs. Harris were turned in another direction) toward our heroine.

"One half the world, lady," replied the vagrant with an air of mystery, " knows not how the other half lives. We are cared for more perhaps than you dream of, or than I dare divulge—but I was summoned to pronounce the destinies of others, not to speak of myself—the shadow of the prophetess hides from herself the good and the evil which lie in her path, but she sees unclouded the orbit of others."

"Will you look at my hand?" asked Mrs. Harris, "I long to know what awaits me."

"I see without reading the hand—your hopes are raised on the expectation of a rich reward, but whether you will obtain it, or for what service, I cannot say."

"Not with my open palm before your eyes?" asked Mrs. Harris, whose curiosity was aroused.

"The lines are crossed," replied the vagrant, rejecting the proffered hand, "give me a pack of new cards, and I will tell whether he whom you trust will deceive you."

The housekeeper paused for a moment.

"I think I can find a pack," said she slowly, "though the nonsense you wenches utter is not worth the trouble."

And so saying, she left the apartment promising to return in a minute.

CHAPTER XV.

As soon as the housekeeper had quitted the room, the fortune-teller approached the chair in which Constance was sitting, and addressed her with earnestness, and in a tone of sincerity which could not be mistaken. What she was about to say, remarked the gipsy, was not the fruit of occult knowledge, or reading the stars, or any gift of palmistry, but the character of the owner of the house in which she then stood was well known—he was a bad, dissolute man, who had been long discarded by every one whose esteem was of value. The woman was a worthless wretch, the very counterpart of her master, and when two such characters were found acting in concert, it was evidently with a view to some piece of villany. But a short time since, and this house was a wretched dismantled edifice, falling to ruin under the care of a poor gardener who lived in an adjoining cottage. The tenantless rooms oft afforded shelter to her tribe. Of a sudden the captain is found repairing his deserted mansion, filling it with some ten or a dozen domestics, placing over them a woman who had been engaged in disgraceful and dishonourable occupations. The house is renovated, the appointments are made, and everything accomplished in entire secresy.

"I see you here, lady, treated like a prisoner," continued the gipsy, "and without looking as far as the stars, do I speak false in saying that all these preparations were made to entrap you, and these servants are mustered to prevent a rescue?"

"How know you that I am a prisoner?" demanded Constance, who was exceedingly struck with the remarks of the vagrant.

"Look at those bars," replied the girl, pointing to the barricaded windows, " our people saw them placed there, and wondered for what intent. The mystery is now solved."

"Then you are sent here as a spy by your tribe?"

"I will be your friend, lady, if you will suffer me. We bear no good will to Captain Henderson for injuries done to us of old."

Constance reflected that the girl could have no motive—at least she could imagine none—for deceiving her, but many causes might exist for hostility between the tribe and the owner of a property on which they had confessedly committed many trespasses, if not depredations. Perhaps they resented being driven from comfortable quarters by the re-occupation of the manor-house. As this idea gained ground, hope grew apace. A channel was unexpectedly opened by which she might communicate the locality of her confinement,—and such a communication being once established, freedom must necessarily follow.

" Tell my friends that I am suffering a cruel imprisonment in this horrid place," exclaimed Constance, rising from the chair, " and you shall have as much gold as you ask for."

" Write down their names, and where they live. For myself I care not for gold, but our people will expect a reward."

" A hundred guineas—more if they wish it. But alas! I have neither paper nor ink—they are too cunning for that."

The gipsy flung down a playing card, and requested our heroine to scratch, with a point of a pair of scissors, the name and abode of her friends.

With a hand trembling with emotion, Constance did as requested, and handed the card to the gipsy, who placed it carefully in her bosom.

" How far am I from London ?" asked the captive.

" More than seventy miles," was the reply, " but hark! I hear the woman on the stairs."

The girl ran to the door and listened. Returning to the table she added—

" I was mistaken—she is still searching for the cards, which are here," and with a smile she produced, from under her cloak, the pack, which she confessed to have purloined from the parlour, in order that the housekeeper might be delayed in the fruitless search, and so afford the opportunity of a private conference with the lady above-stairs.

" This is a lone place—on the sea coast," continued the girl, " there is no house nor village for many miles—but fear not lady! no harm shall come."

At this instant, footsteps on the stairs were audible, and the girl had barely time to caution the young lady not to feel alarm if she heard any unusual noise, or saw any unexpected or startling object, as such were more likely to proceed from friend than foe, and might possibly prove a signal from the tribe, when Mrs. Harris entered angry and disconcerted.

The cards were gone, she remarked, could not be found, although she had seen them in their place in the morning. Something was sure to be missed, she added, whenever a gipsy entered a house.

The girl smiled mysteriously at Constance, and then addressing the housekeeper, said that the loss of the cards mattered not, she might possibly do without them. By a little management, and adroit flattery, the good humour of Mrs. Harris was restored, and the vagrant proceeded to lay bare the secrets of futurity, promising the housekeeper a favourable result to the business which lay nearest to her heart.

Constance was her next patient. Her path, she said, was chequered with good and evil, and it depended very much on her own tact and prudence whether she would be happy or miserable. There was an old man, of whom let her beware— he meditated mischief, from which the only chance of escape was by the interference of a man much younger. Other predictions she uttered, and other suggestions she proposed, the tendency of which were plainly perceptible to Constance. In fact, the burthen of the whole was an admonition to beware of the Earl of Headington, and to regard Captain Henderson in the light of an honourable man, disposed to thwart the evil course of the dissolute nobleman.

To avoid the suspicion of any secret understanding between herself and the gipsy, Constance pretended to tire of the girl's talk, and she was accordingly dismissed.

" They are sad thieves both indoors and out," observed Mrs. Harris, after her return from watching the gipsy beyond the premises. " I am sure the wench has stolen the cards—but believe it or not, they certainly possess the secret of futurity."

Constance smiled, but made no reply.

Left to herself, the meditations of our heroine were of a happier cast. Despondency had fled—fancy pictured friends hastening to her rescue, and the discomfiture and disgrace of the earl and his agent.

Henderson, who had yielded to Mrs. Harris's suggestion of employing the gipsy-girl to throw the influence of her pretended occult science in his favour, rather from an impression that female tact ought not to be disregarded, than from any strong conviction of the potency of the scheme, was however, anxious to test the merits of the vagrant's agency. He solicited an interview, which our heroine did not refuse.

The captain was both surprised and puzzled with his reception. He had expected more weeping, more despair, more lamentation or entreaty, or on the other hand, a torrent of fiery indignation and angry invective. For either case he was prepared. These were states of feeling which he knew how to arrest and controul, and to march secretly to his object while pretending sympathy with the sufferer. But the calmness of Le Raincy left him without a theme for discourse. She uttered no complaint, neither did she give vent to indignation or scorn, nor even make appeals to his sense of justice or honour. Her calmness arose from a feeling of security—she felt her hope lay beyond his reach. He was cut off from every mode of recommending himself—he could not condole with grief of which there appeared no trace, neither could he deprecate the anger which, if felt, was not expressed. Nor was afforded him the opportunity, which he coveted, of offering his protection against the perils which the captive was threatened He had committed a great wrong—had struck a heavy blow at the peace of our heroine—and was constrained (to his great mortification) to abide the odium of his actions. He retired from the meeting baffled and disconcerted, and was forced to confess to himself—and his intellect was too robust and masculine to attempt to evade the confession—that her behaviour placed him in this position, that his only feasible attempt to gain her esteem must commence by reparation of the wrong he had committed. But to set her unconditionally at liberty, was totally inconsistent with the object he had in view—'twas surrendering the only hold by which he trusted to attain his ends.

Next day, and the one following were fraught with no better success. Obliged to conceal his angry mood from Le Raincy, he vented his ill-humour on the housekeeper.

Mrs. Harris, he said, might talk as she liked, but for his part, he could form no other opinion than that Mademoiselle Le Raincy, the pattern of modesty, was ardently desiring the arrival of the earl.

Mrs. Harris very calmly reminded him that his opinion of the modesty and character of Miss Le Rancy was so exalted, that independently of every consideration of wealth or income, he would (as he had avowed) feel honoured by a marriage with the lady.

"Yes—true—true I said so—but I know not what plans or plots you may have matured—I do not say it is so, but for aught I know, I may owe my cold reception to some new idea of Mrs. Harris, who may repent her contract under the expectation of making more by betraying to the earl certain remarks which were uttered."

If the housekeeper had even been guilty of the treachery imputed to her in this speech, she could scarcely have failed to resent the charge—but she had, in fact, held faithful to her engagements with the disappointed captain, and felt keenly his unmerited taunts.

Before such a charge was preferred, retorted Mrs. Harris, it would be well for those who made it, to examine whether the failure of success did not rest with them. The captain was not a young man. She had not divulged his age directy or indirectly, but age cannot always be concealed. His character might not stand so high as it did once—those who had lost money by him at play, or tradesmen who suffered by unpaid bills—had tongues which could not be silenced. And it was quite as fair to presume that Miss Le Raincy had imbibed some prejudice from what she had heard in London, to his disadvantage, as that his ill-luck was the result of treachery. If captain Henderson would reflect calmly, he would perceive that both himself and the housekeeper had committed themselves with respect to their right honourable employer, and that their only chance of extrication, consisted in carrying out their original compact. If that were broken, there remained for Mrs. Harris but one mode of procedure— to confess to his lordship the duplicity of which she had been guilty, and take the chance of his forgiveness. Henderson was again humbled—he had given his bond—he was committed beyond redemption—so he yielded to the urgencies of the situation, and confessed that he had been hasty and in error, and craved pardon.

CHAPTER XVI.

MEANWHILE, hope deferred renewed the despondency of Constance. She feared that her gipsy friend had forgotten her, or that the tribe would not interfere, or that the card on which was written the address of the Benningtons was lost. It was true, that only two days and a half had elapsed, and as the emissary of the gipsies would probably travel to London on foot, another day was not too much to allot to the period when she might look for aid. She was also disappointed in not receiving a signal, or other communication, which she was told to look for. In truth, the mind of our heroine was in a state to be affected by the slightest untoward casualty. The tenor of Captain Henderson's language; reiterated praises of his generosity and noble nature from the lips of Mrs. Harris, aided by hints afforded by the gipsy-girl, enabled Constance to penetrate the schemes of the captain. Indeed, he could make no progress in his addresses without disclosing his real views, by which our heroine could not fail to understand that she had no chance of escape from the earl but by giving a willing ear to the suit of his agent.

In the height of this perplexity, the arrival of his lordship was announced by the housekeeper. The ardour of his passion led him to forget the gathering infirmities of approaching old age, and the journey from London was performed without pause or delay. It was evening when he arrived; and he was so much wearied that he was obliged to retire to rest, and forego the delight of beholding the fair prisoner whom he had encaged. Constance had, therefore, ample time to prepare for the visit. At breakfast she received a perfumed billet, in which he craved permission to throw himself at her feet, and apologised for not having done so on the previous evening, which he attributed to the late hour of arrival.

She was aware it were idle to interdict his approach, so she made no attempt to prevent it. Arrayed in a new coat of peach-coloured velvet, hat under arm, and bouquet in hand, the old beau entered the apartment. All that the perfumer, the milliner, the tailor could do was accomplished.

"What happiness is mine!" exclaimed the voluptuary, approaching Constance. "I have travelled in haste—post-haste—from the court, and believe me, mademoiselle, when I assure you, that although I left St. James's with my heart deeply smitten with the charms of the assembled beauties of England, yet every impression is effaced when I enter your presence."

Constance listened to the address with calmness, even indifference.

"Unhappy man that I am!" he exclaimed, "what have I done to deserve this coldness? Have you been neglected? Forgive the immurement—it was public business alone—the business of my sovereign, whom I could not disobey, which detained me in London.'

Constance replied, that as her lengthened imprisonment was, by his lordship's confession, caused only by his being detained in London, she was indeed glad of his arrival. She earnestly implored him to restore her to liberty, and the misery she had experienced herself, as well as the anxiety her friends must have endured, should all be forgiven.

"Mademoiselle Le Raincy," said the old gentleman, in a tone of the most insinuating gallantry, "overlooks the anxiety of the most devoted of her friends."

Our heroine remarked, with asperity, that she would not affect to misunderstand his lordship. She was the child of misfortune. The loss, at an early age, of her natural protectors, threw her on her own resources—she became, in experience, a woman whilst yet a child. His lordship might judge then of the effect of such addresses. There was but one condition on which she would consent to listen to him—free her from restraint—convey her to the nearest town or village, and she might begin to entertain for the Earl of Headington the respect which was due to a gentleman of his station.

"You have no pity," exclaimed the earl.

"I retort the charge," cried Constance with indignation.

"Forgive me, fair lady," uttered his lordship, with an imploring glance, as he dropped on one knee, "if I have committed violence to your feelings, or your liberty, let my excuse be, that I have worshipped you. If love is sometimes the author of violence, he well knows how to repair the wrong."

Constance observed that the language of comedy might possibly make an impression on the fancy of some country-maiden, but to one like herself, familiar with the stage, and unhappily, familiar with grief and misfortune, such an address created no other impression than contempt. She trusted that his lordship would have the good sense and politeness to perceive the incongruity, between his conduct and the style of his language—that the path was open to retrace his steps, and she hoped his lordship would, by to-morrow morning, avail himself of the offer of compromise and forgiveness.

With these remarks she arose and retired to her chamber. The disappointed nobleman heard the bolt turned upon him ere he had recovered his feet, or his surprise at the repulse.

"These stage-wenches," muttered his lordship, as he slowly retired, "represent so often ladies of quality, that, by ——; they end in believing themselves to be such. But her pride shall be tamed."

A sharp colloquy ensued next morning between the earl and Henderson. His lordship wanted to know in what way they had behaved to Le Raincy, to cause her to feel and express so much indignation. His orders were, that no means nor expenses were to be spared in order to prove to her the superiority of her new abode to her residence at the milliner's. The captain retorted, that the fault, if any, attached to his lordship, not to himself. He had observed the most respectful behaviour, but Mademoiselle Le Raincy was a girl of spirit and intelligence, and his lordship would find that fine words would have but little weight. If the earl wished to make an impression, he must condescend to speak on business. Let him propose, as he contemplated, a handsome settlement—a coach and a pair of horses was a picture of more weighty rhetoric than the most honeyed words.

"But the girl treats me as though I were some old, ugly Turkish tyrant, and she, forsooth, a princess in captivity; nay, she sneers at me, but I'll have revenge on the hussy—the cutter has dropped anchor in the bay."

Henderson conjured his lordship not to lose temper; affairs, he said, were progressing favourably, and would have proved much more agreeable if his lordship had studied, with any care, the character of Le Raincy.

"Give me a lesson, most sapient captain," cried Headington, in a tone of irony, "and I'll try its effects."

Henderson remarked, that his lordship was at liberty to jest with him as much as he pleased, but he would advise him whilst he remained in the same frame of mind, not to visit Le Raincy. His lordship, he said, was chafed and angry, and therefore in an improper state to renew his visit. His advice was to the effect that his lordship should take a drive along the coast, or sail over the bay, which would tranquillize his spirits, which had been thrown off their equilibrium by the fatigue of travel and the discomfiture of his reception.

Headington could not but acknowledge that he had mistaken the character of Le Raincy. He yielded to the captain's suggestion. The horses were ordered to the door, and he was driven off to enjoy the refreshing ocean-breeze, and take council with himself in respect to a fresh attack on the unfortunate captive.

From his own experience the captain was not at all surprised at the ill-success of the peer. Neither was the advice which he proffered his lordship, such as, if carried into effect, likely to promote the earl's views. He was persuaded that Le Raincy would reject with indignation, or laugh to scorn, the pecuniary offers of his lordship, based, as they were, on the stipulation of a dishonourable connection. Even for himself, he believed that there was but one means of success; but that was all-potent. She was totally, and without hope of release, in their power; and were she but shown that her only chance of escape from ruin and dishonour

No. 9,

was by an honourable marriage with himself, she would not hesitate to accept his offers.

But there was no time to lose. The crisis of his fate was at hand. He did not stay to seek council of his coadjutor, but hurried to the apartments of Le Raincy; but our heroine refused to see him unless in the presence of Mrs. Harris. The housekeeper was accordingly summoned.

The urgency of the occasion lent eloquence to the captain's discourse. Both his tone and his arguments carried weight, for much of what he said was true. He described all the precautions taken by Lord Headington to ensure the accomplishment of his wishes; the loneliness of the house; the number of servants, and their devotedness to his interests. The captive could number but two friends, Mrs. Harris and himself; and were she only disposed to listen to the captain's suit, it would open an honourable door of escape.

Constance whose hopes were buoyed up with expectation of aid or rescue from her gipsy-friend, and who judged that sufficient time had elapsed to convey to her friends a knowledge of the place where she was confined, listened to Henderson's remarks with indifference.

"You know not, mademoiselle, the extent of the peril which surrounds you," cried the captain, "let us walk to the other side of the house."

He led the way to an apartment which over-looked the sea, and pointing to a window, bade her examine the prospect. A bare, lonely coast stretched either way, for many a mile, without a hut, house or dwelling of any kind. Riding at anchor, in a small bay, beneath the windows, rocked a handsomely-rigged cutter. Henderson informed her that the craft was his lordship's property, and was manned by a crew who were prepared to do, without scruple, whatever he required. Foreseeing the possibility of Le Raincy's obstinacy, he had ordered round the cutter with the intent, if she proved wilfully perverse, of carrying her on board. In such an event, it would be three months or more ere she would see her own country.

The captain proved his sagacity. Poor Constance was stunned with the threatened death-blow of her hopes; her spirits failed, and she sank, in a swoon, into the arms of Mrs. Harris. She was carried back to her apartment, and gradually revived under the assiduous care of the housekeeper and Mr. Henderson. The latter, when he expressed his deep sympathy for her distress, did not misrepresent his feelings; but self-interest was too powerful to admit the unrestrained action of generous impulse. Circumstances, he declared to Constance, when she had recovered her senses, had made him the slave and dependant of the Earl of Headington; but on the condition he had named, and on no other, he was willing to sacrifice the interests of his patron, and, by so doing, effect the rescue of Mlle. Le Raincy. She had better, he said, take one hour to decide—longer time would not be afforded, as the earl's return would, in all probability, preclude the chance of the captain being afterward of service to the unfortunate lady.

Left to her own reflections, for the first time, Constance bestowed serious attention on Henderson's proposals. The alternative was dreadful to contemplate. The facts spoke but too plainly, or she would have accounted the captain's report a fabrication. It was but too evident for what purpose the cutter lay at anchor, and how could she help herself aboard, or, indeed, prevent herself being carried on board?

If the gipsy's estimate of the captain's character had not struck a deep impression on her mind, it is probable that her desperate situation, aided by his apparent candour, might have influenced, materially, her decision. But, meanwhile, as the scales vibrated in the beam, as she weighed the chances of the cruel alternative, she heard the sound of carriage-wheels. The idea of rescue flashed on her mind; her friends were at hand! She flew to the door—alas! it was fastened on the outside as usual. From the window nothing was visible but the mass of green foliage which approximated on that side, so closely to the house.

A stir was heard below—a few minutes elapsed—when Mrs. Harris entered the apartment, announcing in an angry, reproachful tone, and with startling abruptness, that her hour of grace was shortened, and her chance of escape irretrievably ruined by the return of his lordship earlier than was expected. Instead of the captain's honourable conduct and proposals, she might prepare for the fate to which, by her obstinacy, she had shown herself so callous.

CHAPTER XVII.

CONSTANCE was soon relieved of the presence of the house-keeper, who was summoned to attend to the preparation of an early dinner for his lordship.

Our heroine, left to her own reflections, knew not how to act, or what to do. Henderson's object was palpable enough—he was, or had been, a dissolute spend-thrift: nor was it out of keeping with the character of such a man, that having engaged in a scheme of infamy, he should seek clandestinely to betray his employer, in order to suit his selfish ends. It had not escaped the penetration of Le Raincy, that the housekeeper was in the interest of the captain, and that the policy of both mercenaries was to thwart the earl, solely with a view to their own aggrandisement. Constance had hoped, by keeping both the earl and his agent in check, to make the treachery of the latter subservient to her safety. But the alarm of Mrs. Harris plainly foretold that affairs were fast hastening to a crisis. The vision of that dreadful cutter—the horror of being carried on board, and taken she knew not where—awoke a paroxysm of despair. Where were the kind friends who should have flown to her rescue? Was it possible that one of her station and fame could be carried off from London, without exciting the indignation of the town, and causing the most rigid search!

Whilst tortured with these thoughts, her eye was attracted to the window. She beheld something moving to and fro on the outside. At another season, she might have been frightened, but her mind was intent on the chance of her being rescued, and she had not forgotten the promise of the gipsy. She ran to the window, and opening it gently, contrived to get her head between the bars. Below stood her friend, the fortune-teller, in her hand a long sapling, to the point of which was affixed a handkerchief, the object which Constance had beheld in motion.

" I know you are alone," said the gipsy in a loud whisper, " your enemies are all together in the parlour round the corner, and I have much to say."

Le Raincy, in despair, expressed her fears that she would not be able to come up stairs unseen by the servants, or mayhap the watchful housekeeper, and moreover, she of the red-cloak was out of the good graces of Mrs. Harris, who accused her of stealing the cards.

" I did take them," said the girl, laughing, " as you know—but there is no need, for our purpose, that I should come in at the door like honest folk."

To the astonishment of the captive, the girl climbed readily up the wall, and brought her sun-burnt, laughing features on a level with the pale face of Le Raincy.

Constance could not help uttering an expression of surprise.

" Is it easier, lady," said the girl, " to read the stars than to climb this wall? But there is no magic in the feat."

The vagrant proceeded to acquaint the fair prisoner, that the ready ascent was owing to the contrivance of her male friends, who had duly reconnoitred the premises and chiselled the wall so as to render the escalade practicable and easy. Nor was the present attempt the first which had been made.

" Night and day, fair lady, we watch over you—"

" How !" exclaimed Constance, who was shocked at the idea of being exposed, at will, to the gaze of a whole tribe of gipsies. Nor was her apprehension allayed when she was informed, that yesterday the gipsy's brother made the ascent, but he could not speak, as Mrs. Harris was in the room. Indeed, so afraid was the young man that he was discovered, that he narrowly escaped breaking his neck by flinging himself to the ground, from whence he escaped behind the shrubbery.

"Stay, stay!" cried Constance, in perturbation, "this reminds me that you may be discovered now, but I have the keys."

Mrs. Harris, as before mentioned, had surrendered to Le Raincy the keys of both apartments, by which she could, whenever she desired, lock out unwelcome visitors. She ran across the room and locked the door, taking care to throw her handkerchief over the key-hole.

"And so your brother wished to speak to me?"

The girl replied, that her brother had been charged to say, that a trusty messenger was sent to London to reveal the place where she was detained in durance; and that his return, perhaps in company with aid, was hourly expected. He ought, according to their notion of the journey, to have presented himself at the encampment yesterday. If mishap had befallen him, they would doubtless have heard of it, as they had friends everywhere.

Constance expressed the warmest acknowledgment of the services which this poor vagrant girl and her tribe were performing on her behalf, but she feared, after all the trouble taken, that aid would arrive too late.

"We never break our promise," uttered the girl, with an air of offended dignity.

"Have you seen the cutter at anchor in the bay?" asked Constance.

"Yes; we have all seen it."

"Do you know to whom it belongs?"

"To your enemies," replied the gypsy.

"Could you and your friends prevent my being carried on board?"

"No! no!" responded the girl, shaking her head, "there are too many men in the house and in the ship."

"Then it's likely I may be forced on board to-morrow in spite of the good-will of your tribe."

"Heaven forbid!" cried the girl.

"That is the fate I am threatened with—if my friends arrive not, I am indeed lost."

"Two of our tribe have been sailors," said the gipsy, after a few moments consideration, "if we cannot prevent, in time, your being removed, rest assured, lady, we will not desert you—you will have friends on the voyage."

There was a pause, during which each seemed wrapped in thought.

"Yes!" continued the girl, her eyes sparkling with fire, "fear not, you are safe. I see everything brightly. They shall be run aground, or carried into port, when the others are asleep."

The conference was cut short by a loud rattling of the door.

"Haste, haste!" whispered Constance, placing her fingers on the hand of the gipsy, "there is some one knocking."

"Farewell," cried the fortune-teller.

"Farewell," responded our heroine.

As she descended, the gipsy pressed the fingers of Le Raincy against her lips. In another instant the window was closed, and the prisoner, rubbing her eyes, as though she had been suddenly awakened from slumber, hastened to the door.

Whilst Constance was indulging the most melancholy forebodings, her persecutors were faring sumptuously below. Dinner was over—the earl and his coadjutor were seated, opposite to each other, with the generous Burgundy between them. It was circulating rather quickly, for his lordship was out of temper, and sought consolation in the goblet.

"The hussy!" exclaimed Lord Headington, dashing his glass on the table with a vehemence which severed the stem, "and what am I to do now after all this expense? Return to town again a baffled fool? She spurns me—sets me at defiance—yet I could worship for ever that angry eye and curling lip, if I thought they would yield."

Now, Henderson had no desire they should ever yield; indeed, he had a steadfast conviction, that Constance would spurn the earl to the last, spite of threats or promises, or both united.

The captain stood in the singular position, that he could give the most palatable advice to his lordship without fear that his own interests would be damaged by its being acted on. Whilst acting the part of a zealous panderer, he effectually screened himself from the remotest suspicion of treachery; and yet he meditated, schemed, and planned the overthrow of his patron's unbridled wishes. The more pressing the earl's importunities the greater the disgust of Mademoiselle Le Raincy; yet, at the same time, the more alarming would grow her fears, till she were glad to throw herself into the arms of the captain, and so save herself from the violence of the earl! This was the basis of his policy.

" 'Tis your lordship's own fault that you enjoy not better fortune," observed our adventurer, with a sneer only half-concealed, "the field is all your own, and yet like some Hampshire squire, who has never spoken to a girl beyond the bounds of the village, you wait for consent! For consent! Why you might wait till dooms-day."

" You use the freedom of your own house, sir," remarked Headington, who was nettled with the tone of the captain's observations, " you were wont to observe a different line."

" Forgive my zeal if it outrun discretion," rejoined the captain. " I am anxious that your lordship should retain your reputation as a leader of the *beau-monde*."

" Well, well; I was snappish."

" 'Tis useless, my lord, undertaking a siege with all the formalities—take her to the window—show her the yacht, and let her understand, that if she do not receive your lordship's attentions under this humble roof, that her abode would be transferred to the cabin of yon craft, and I'll answer for the result."

" Your advice is good, captain; indeed, I have observed that the advice of most men of any capacity is good, yet it is often hard to follow, yet I'll try it."

" Do so, my lord; I am about to ride over to the town for letters, and I expect to find on my return, that my Lord Headington is himself again."

The captain arose from table, and after jocularly expressing a hope, that if his lordship really felt inclined to abandon the pursuit, that he would make a tried friend happy, by resigning the field to him, quitted the parlour, and ordered his horse to the door.

A sneer from his own dependant stung the nobleman acutely. The fellow was laughing at him, and certainly when it was considered how many months' preparation, and how much money it cost to carry off an opera-dancer to the sea-side for change of air—and all to end in being scolded by the wench, and sneered at by the agent and tool—there was food for laughter. " I'll prove conquerer," he muttered, to himself " or take the rascal's hint, and hie back to Hanover-square."

His lordship pushed aside the bottle, and after a momentary survey of himself in the mirror, strode up stairs to visit his prisoner.

CHAPTER XVIII.

THE visit of the earl broke off the interview between Constance and the gipsy. When the former opened the door, she was startled at the changed demeanour of his lordship. In place of the habitual bland simper which hovered over the features, she beheld a fixed stern aspect which foreboded evil, and recalled the words of Mrs. Harris. The eye, never bright, was glazed and immovable. A thickening of the speech and a slight unsteadiness of gait revealed the extent of his

Bacchanalian sacrifices. Constance regretted that she had unfastened the door, but it was too late to exclude the unwelcome visiter. Her hand was still on the lock, and she was dubious whether she could not escape from the apartment. Probably he divined her thoughts.

"Pardon me," he said, leading her toward a seat, "I have much to say."

As soon as her hand was disengaged, he turned round—more nimbly than she could have expected from a man of his years and premature debility—and closing the door, locked it, and removed the key.

Le Raincy flew to prevent him, but she was too late, and retreated again to escape from his outstretched arms.

"Our conference must be private," cried Headington, resuming his usual simper.

"But not with the door locked," cried Constance, "I expected better treatment from one who boasts of public employment from his sovereign."

"But stratagem is permitted in both love and war. A mere trick of Cupid—but hear me, mademoiselle, and then confess whether the cruel endurance you suffer here is not the fruit of your own cruel obstinacy."

Constance made an impatient gesture that he should proceed to say what he had to utter.

The earl objected that his sense of politeness would not permit him to keep a lady standing—he entreated her to be seated, that he might be more at ease in what he had to say.

Le Raincy replied, that if his sense of courtesy would allow him to act the unmanly part of turning the key of a lady's apartment, and holding her a prisoner against her will, his gallantry could not be very deeply outraged by seeing his prisoner stand.

"Wit and beauty joined!" said Headington with a deep sigh, "how can I escape the chains which are woven round me? What is it to be imprisoned in these chambers, compared to the torments which you make me suffer, cruel one?"

The perception of the ludicrous so natural to histrionic artists, obtruded on Constance spite of her distresses. Who could listen to the enfeebled voluptuary, with form and features stamped with decay, and hear him descant on the pressure of the chains which bound his heart, and of the tricks which Cupid inspirited him to perform, without contempt and (at least) internal laughter? The earl was eloquent in depicting his misery. If the fair enchantress would but be merciful, all the wealth he could command he would lay at her feet. He was prepared to execute a settlement, the amount of which she should herself name—an equipage, a house—servants—nothing should be wanting.

All these fine offers Le Raincy treated with scorn, and threatened him with the vengeance of the law, and of her friends, if he did not set her at liberty.

"There is one infliction mademoiselle has not threatened me with," said his lordship, "but which I should really smart under. What care I for the foolish anger of men-milliners and stage-managers?"

"And what sir, is the punishment you dread?" asked the captive, with—it must be confessed—some inkling of curiosity.

"Ridicule—madame—ridicule—if I let you escape after all the pains I have taken, I never dare show my face among men of my own quality. But I'll die first before you depart from my power without first consenting to my terms."

Having fallen from the tone of courtesy, which thinly veiled his rude villany, he spoke in plain language of the impossibility of her escape—that the house in which she was now lodged, was a lone tenement several miles from any other homestead, and a very considerable distance from the line of travel or traffic. So effectual were his precautions that it was impossible her friends could discover the retreat, but he did not trust to that chance, as his yacht lay at anchor before the house, and he had men enough, both in the house and in the yacht to carry her on board spite of any resistance offered by friends. If she would not yield to his conditions, he would set sail with her forthwith to the south of Italy, or the Plantations, or other quarter which he deemed most inaccessible and secluded.

Constance pretended to hear him unmoved, though in reality she was driven to despair.

"You do not speak, fair charmer —how happy could I be, did I hear one word of hope! see one sign of relenting."

Le Raincy glanced vaguely round the apartment, but she spoke not. Indignanation witheld her replying to his insults, yet she was undecided.

"Silence, sweetheart, gives consent—I read it in your eyes."

The earl approached and attempted to throw his arms around her—she could not retreat, as a table stood in the way, bnt she snatched up a pair of sharp-pointed scissors which for some time she had been eyeing as a friendly weapon at need, and plunged them into his side.

Headington staggered to a chair, against which he leaned, whilst Constance, amazed at her own act, looked on speechless. But when she beheld his apparel blood-stained, and his face assume an expression of intense bodily pain, she cried aloud for help—declaring in her excitement that she had killed the earl.

" No, no ! a mere scratch," uttered the wounded man, " raise no alarm I pray you—I entreat—a mere bodkin, nothing more—all will be well in an hour. I'll have revenge for this by——. To-morrow morning, vixen, you shall be safe on board the cutter—and then—— "

He staggered to the door, unlocked it—and poor Constance was once more alone, a prisoner. Through the sagacity of his valet, Edmonstone had struck on the right track of pursuit, though he had as yet failed to discover the spot, or even the neighbourhood where the fair danseuse was held in durance.

In the reign of the second George, travelling was a more serious and complicated undertaking than in the present century. It was a fine morning in June—the locality, the southern portion of Hampshire, that Arthur followed by his servant. also mounted, might be seen riding forth like a knight-errant of old intent on deeds of chivalry. Sometimes the servant rode beside his master, and their discourse oft turned on their own ability to resist successfully the attacks of armed highwaymen, with which the entire kingdom was infested, and who oft-times exhibited the utmost audacity in attacking a stage full of passengers, or a gentleman's coach.

Arthur could, it is true, boast of his swift sure-footed gelding, but then the animal carried a heavy cumbersome weight. Saddle-bags, containing changes of linen and other necessaries—a pair of large holster-pistols concealed by the said bags from the prying eyes of strangers, yet ready for instant service—a large loose coat behind to cover during a storm, the trim-fashioned apparel of the gay merchant—all these, it is true, were hindrances in either flying from or resisting the attacks of the predatory gentry whose war-cry was—stand and deliver— but these disadvantages were counter-balanced by the size and athletic form of the rider, the open courageous bearing, ad eye looking fiercer beneath the broad travelling-hat. For whip he carried a tapering thong—the handle of iron, welded into a leaden socket, heavy enough to dismount the best-seated ruffian between London and the Land's-End, and growing so " small by degrees and beautifully less," that the other extremity might have swept a fly from the nag's ear without hurting the insect. Francis was equally well-accoutred.

But peril comes not when courted, or when best provided against. Nothing was encountered which might be called an adventure. Farmers hurrying to market, or coming leisurely from it—fat country parsons on ambling nags pacing quietly to make visits of consultation, or exaction of tithes—these were in plenty ; and occasionally a yeoman's daughter with laughing cheeks and bright eyes, riding in company with father or brother, not displeased to exchange a smile with the handsome traveller, and with enough coquetry to betray it. Sometimes the slow moving wagon was overtaken—that vast receptacle of merchandise, piled high with goods of every description, protected by arching roof of canvass impervious to wet. In the rear where the opening drapery admitted the light and beeeze, were distinguishable, comfortably esconced on a bedding of hay, the humble travellers of both sexes too poor to transport themselves, and their luggage to the metropolis in vehicles of a better class. Sometimes a-head of the team of eight horses (whose jingling bells gave timely notice of approach to the ostler or "mine host,") encouraging the cattle to surmount a hill—but still oftener in the rear, chatting with passengers, whose scanty pay was his perquisite, leaving the horses to their own guidance, was seen the wagoner with round, white frock, black hat and whip, which played like a trout-rod whisked across a brook.

A pleasant mode of travelling, we have oft imagined, in that same waggon with its tilt-roof and hay carpet! Its leisurely speed of three miles per hour, affording opportunity of walking or riding as suited inclination—loitering behind to cut a hazel stick, or chat with a rustic beauty whose path lay across the meadows—and with the sweet certainty of being able to overtake the tortoise-like conveyance. Often have we expressed a wish, in our younger days, when joyous health, a bright sun over head, and an indifferently well stored purse were our contented portion, to try the experiment. How pleasant such must be ! as we have oft repeated to an acquaintance—indeed, very pleasant (was the reply) when one found a pretty fellow-traveller.

From scenes such as we have described, and speculations whether that day's journey would reveal the spot where Constance was imprisoned, they were aroused about noon by a faint scream, but from whom, or whence it proceeded, they could not discover, as the road, about a furlong in advance, intersected another, and the continuation of both was hidden by a sharp angle.

The faint clue obtained by Francis, and by which they were guided in their search, did not warrant the belief, that the hour had arrived to do battle for the imprisoned damsel, yet the cry was a cry of distress. Buttoning his coat, rising for an instant in the stirrups, and dropping firmly in the saddle—whilst he suffered the heavy-hilted whip to slide through the grasp till he held it rather short of the middle, so held a most destructive weapon, he clapped spurs to the nag, and bidding Francis follow, shot by the corner to the rescue of the sufferer.

He beheld a stage coach drawn across the middle of the road—the passengers both inside and out in confusion—the reins had fallen from the coachman's grasp , and were lying on the haunches of the wheel horses—the whip was half-hidden in the dust, and Jehu himself appeared in a paroxysm of fright, which was communicated to the passengers under his charge, who were reluctantly engaged in feeling for their purses. Two well-mounted horsemen were in the act of demanding their money—the one taking in hand the outside travellers, the other with protruded pistol frightening the occupants of the interior. The scream proceeded from a lady inside who had fainted—her male companions were shouting for air, bidding the ruffian stand away from the window, or he would be the death of the lady, and at the same time were searching in every pocket but the right one for their purses.

"Quick ! quick ! ladies and gentlemen," cried the highwayman, jarring his pistol against the panel.

"Yes! yes !" cried an elderly gentleman trembling from head to foot, and who held a thick oaken walking-stick firmly—between his knees.

Meanwhile the other knight of the road, who had to look after the horses, the coachman and the outsiders, suffered two of the latter to escape, which they effected by dropping from the off-side of the stage, and crawling through a gap in the hedge.

Arthur would have struck to the earth the horseman engaged at the stage-window, had not his companion, who heard the stranger's approach, warned him barely in time to save his head from a blow, the effects of which he must have long remembered, if indeed he could have survived the concussion.

"Stay your hand, sir !" cried Jehu, jumping in alarm from the box, "it is all a mistake—it is a freak, sir."

"A what ?" exclaimed Arthur, glancing from the coachman to the assailants ; "are you rogues or honest men ?"

The two highwaymen were abashed and disconcerted, and surveyed each other without speaking—Jehu was obliged to be, a second time, spokesman.

"Hold off, Sir," he cried, "it is all a frolic—these two gentlemen are proprietors of the coach——"

"The deuce they are !" shouted the elderly gentleman from the inside, at the same time opening the door, and letting himself out.   He appeared very suddenly to have recovered his valour, for he brandished the oaken towel stoutly ; the two outsiders, creeping from their place of concealment, sprung suddenly on the rider who had saved his companion from Arthur's whip, dismounted and disarmed him,

ARTHUR TRYS THE GIPSIES SKILL TO FIND CONSTANCE.

to which proceeding he offered no opposition, which so encouraged the elderly gentleman and the other passengers, that they made an attempt on his comrade with the same success.

Meanwhile, Arthur, to whom the whole proceeding was strange and grotesque, could not have refrained from laughter at the unexpected valour of the passsengers, had not the scream still rung in his ear.   He could not help it—but, however improbable, something whispered that he should discover his playmate Constance. Looking through the window he beheld a lady still reclining with closed eyes— but alas ! it was not Constance,

No. 10.

"Some water here," shouted Edmonstone, "haste one of you to the brook."

"No! no!" cried the lady, starting up, "I am quite recovered."

"I never witnessed so rapid a recovery," thought Arthur, but was too polite to say so.

The fair passenger was on what is called the wrong side of forty, by which is meant that side which can boast of most wisdom, caution, worldly experience and freedom from errors—still she blushed at finding her face so near that of a handsome stranger—blushed as though she were on the youthful side of the before-mentioned age, and to the offer of lifting her from the coach, declared in a low voice that she really thought the air would do her good after the alarm.

As the lady was handed out by Arthur, who had gallantly dismounted for the purpose, he heard the elderly gentleman haranguing the abashed stage proprietors with a high hand.

"It is a shameful trick for gentlemen in your station of life—and the poor lady, she may never recover the fright. You owe us all reparation—we will expose you in the newspapers, and ruin the coach. It is well, sirs, for one of you at least, that the young gentleman approached, or this bludgeon," here he shook aloft his walking stick, "and a rogue's head would have come in contact."

"Aye! aye! they both owe their safety to the stranger," cried another voice, "for I was about to shoot the other thief who stood at the horse's heads."

"Shall we duck them in the brook?" asked a third.

"Yes, and serve the coachman the same, he is an accomplice."

"But you must catch him first!" shouted the jolly coachman, who appeared to hold the prowess of the passengers in utter contempt, and put himself into a boxing attitude.

"James! stand back, and keep an insolent tongue quiet," said one of the culprits. Turning to the passengers, he continued, "gentlemen, we are sorry, truly sorry, for what we have done. The fact is, we had been, that is, all the co-partners of the line, partaking of a luncheon together, and—to make short of a troublesome affair, we are not very sober—but we shall be very glad if all present will eat a good dinner at our expense at ——— and forget all that has happened."

This proposal was well-timed, and proved that the larksome proprietor was not so far gone, but that he knew how to appeal very effectually to the sympathies of his auditors. The elderly gentleman proposed that the offer should be accepted, with the condition that both offenders knelt on the bare ground, and begged the company's pardon. This suggestion was demurred to by the would-be highwaymen, as too humiliating, and it was finally agreed that homage should be paid to, and pardon asked only of the lady.

It was proposed that Arthur Edmonstone shold be master of the ceremonies. He was in no mood for foolery, yet he knew not how to refuse, so ordering a box to be removed from the roof of the coach, he caused the lady to be seated, and having previously inquired her name, which she lispingly announced as Miss Priscilla Woodberry, he introduced the culprits severally—Mr. John Thornton and Mr. Harry Lovejoy—to the fair Priscilla, suing for pardon, which, with many blushes, and "dear me's," was condescendingly granted. James having acted under superior orders, was dismissed with a slight reprimand.

———

CHAPTER XIX.

WHILST Arthur sat at dinner with the passengers, his servant Francis—as arranged—was busily employed making inquiries. From gossip picked up in the kitchen, combined with his own sources of information, he was of opinion, that they were not distant many miles from the place whither Mademoiselle Le Raincy had been conveyed. Full of hope he hastened to the parlour, and whispered in the ear of his master the pleasing intelligence.

Arthur was indeed glad of any pretext for quitting the company. The fainting heroine of the stage-coach was bent on a conquest—she made continual demands on his politeness and intentions, which he could not shake off without positive incivility. When he announced his intention of riding forward she would not hear of it, and he was only permitted to depart by giving a pledge, that as he must speedily be overtaken by the stage, that he would keeep it company, so long as the journey permitted.

Arthur was, however, bent on escaping from the toils of the ancient spinster. As soon as he had arrived at a village about half an hour's ride from the town of ————,he dismounted at the inn-door, ordered Francis to stable the horses and bribe the host to inform the passengers, (if the question were asked,) that the travellers they expected to overtake had rode through without alighting. He then wandered carelessly across some meadows, keeping in view an eminence at a short distance, crowned by a tuft of foliage, from whence he was certain of seeing the stage. Crossing a rustic foot-bridge, formed by a single plank, thrown across a brook, he commenced a gentle ascent toward the summit of the hillock. On arriving at the top, he found himself in view of a charming scene. The rich woodland, redolent of balmy scents, was spread out before him, and between the trees he caught occasional glimpses of the not far distant ocean. The effect was exhilirating, and Edmonstone, although deeply anxious for the fate of the fair friend of other days, did not resist the influence of nature; he even for a few moments forgot all the difficulties in his way, and, taking a seat on a grassy mound, resigned himself to the calm and unalloyed pleasure ever to be derived from the contemplation of the beauties of creation by those who look on them with unjaundiced eyes.

Soft and yellow the sunbeams gleamed through the heavy branches of a wood on one side and illumined all its chambers. Through the wide stillness the woodpecker's beak was sometimes heard. The startled partridge broke from his covert with whirring wings, and the gentle robin whistled as he flew silently by. Bees were humming among the flowers, and at a distance, the dash of a little cascade drew the eye to the spot where its shining water turned over a [broken, rock, and fell flashing and foaming through the trees. The forest-looking wood completely filled Edmonstone's imagination. It reminded him of the scenery so well delineated in Ivanhoe, where Robin Hood and the stout friar played their] merry pranks—where the black knight wandered after the tournament, and joined the besiegers in beating down the massive battlements of that amiable gentleman, Front de Bœuf. But here, alas! were no battlements, no giants, no kings in disguise, no wandering knights—nothing but strapping farmer-boys; or a carter occasionally driving along his clumsy waggon, heavily laden with corn.

The search in which he was engaged was not devoid of excitement, and, though fatigued, the mere act of travelling rapidly had not been depressing in its effects. Indeed he began to think, with others, that it is a wholesome thing to be what is commonly termed "kicked about the world; not literally "kicked"—not forcibly propelled by innumerable feet, from village to village, from town to town, or from country to country, which can be neither wholesome nor agreeable; but knocked about, tossed about, irregularly jostled over many leagues of road; sleeping hard and soft, living well when you can, and learning to take what is barely edible and potable ungrumblingly when there is no help for it. Certes, the departure from home and old usages is anything but pleasant, especial'v t the outset. It is a sort of secondary "weaning" which the juvenile has to undergo; but, as after the first process, he is all the healthier and hardier when it is over. In this way, it is a wholesome thing to be tossed about the world; to form odd acquaintance in ships, on the decks of steamboats, and tops of coaches; to pick up temporary companions on turnpikes, or by hedge sides; to see humanity in the rough, and learn what stuff life is made of in different places; to mark the shades and points of distinction in men, manners, customs, cookery, and other important matters, as you stroll along. What an universal toleration it begets. How it improves and enlarges a man's physical and intellectual tastes and capacities! How diminutively local and ridiculously lilliputian seems his former experiences! He is now no longer bigoted to a doctrine or a dish, but can fall in with one, or eat of the other, however strange and foreign, with a facility truly comfortable and commendable ; always, indeed, excepting such doctrines as affect the feelings and sentiments, which he should ever keep " garnered up " in his "heart of hearts" and also always excepting the swallowing of certain substances so very peculiar in themselves, and so strictly national, that the undisciplined palate of the foreigner instinctively and utterly rejects them ; such as the frogs of your Frenchman, the garlic of your Spaniard, the compounds, termed sausages, of your cockney, the haggis of your Scotchman, the train-oil of your Russian, &c.

He has but little of the ardent spirit of boyhood, or the mounting spirit of manhood in him, who can quietly seat himself by his father's hearth, dear though it be, until that hearth, by virtue of inheritance becomes his own, without a wish to see how the world wags beyond the walls of his native town. How mulish and uncompromising he groweth up! How very indocile and incredulous he becometh! To him, localities are truths, right is wrong, and wrong is right, just as they fall in with, or differ from the customs of his district ; and all that is rare, or curious, or strange, or wonderful, or different from what he has been accustomed to, is measured by the petty standard of his own experience, and dogmatically censured or praised accordingly. Such men are incurable, and what is worse, legal nuisances —they can neither be abated by law nor logic.

I like human nature of quite a different pattern from this. A boy, especially, is all the better for a strong infusion of credulity in his composition. He should swallow an hyperbole unhesitatingly, and digest it without difficulty. It is better for a juvenile to be ingenuous than ingenious. It is better for him to study Baron Munchausen than Poor Richard's Maxims. The baron's inventions fertilize his imagination, without injuring his love of truth ; Poor Richard's truisms teach him nothing but that cold, worldly wisdom he is almost sure to learn, and learn too soon. Strong drink is not for babes and sucklings ; neither are miserly, hard-hearted proverbs, " a penny saved is a penny earned," " a groat a day is a pound a year," and such like arithmetical wisdom. Keep it from them. It takes the edge off their young sensibilities, and sets them calculating their charities. They will learn selfishness soon enough, without taking regular lessons. The good Samaritan, honest man, cared not a fig-leaf for such axioms, or he too would have passed by on the other side."

We have travelled much, and beheld, with corporeal eye, many of the scenes and places that looked so surpassingly fair to our inward vision in former times. We have become "familiar with strange faces," and have made friends and acquaintance in far-off countries. But time and the world have done their usual work with us, as with others. We are changed—vilely sophisticated ; the smoke of cities is upon our soul, and innumerable trivial sensualities have imperceptibly clogged the elastic spring of the spirit within us. To enjoy the company of old mother nature now, we must have " all appliances and means to boot ;" be easy and comfortable, neither hungry nor a thirst, instead of seeking her in every form and mood as of yore. But this is the way, more or less, with us all. As we grow up we acquire an unconscious preference for art above nature ; we love the country less, and the town more ; and shady walks and " hedge rows green " are forsaken for well-paved streets and public promenades. We muddle our brains with political economy, and form attachments to newspapers, and distilled and fermented liqors, that it is often difficult to shake off. Oh, the lamentable deterioration of human nature! We are the antipodes (to our disadvantage,) of even the despised caterpillar tribe ; we do not expand from the grub into the butterfly, but degenerate from the butterfly into the grub. When boys, or wingless butterflies, we disport in the free air and sunshine, clad in the hues of health, and as free from care or trouble as the lilies of the field. Every returning day brings animation and enjoyment—

" Flowers in the valley, splendour in the beam,
Health in the gale, and freshness in the stream,"

until the remorseless usuages of the world apprentice us to the doctors, tailors,
lawyers, merchants, shipwrights, sugar-bakers, &c., to be initiated into their
respective mysteries ; we grow up to be sallow, bearded men ; we herd together in
cities—we monotonously slink, day after day, from the dull obscurity of our
dwellings, through dirty lanes and dusky alleys, to our strange occupations, and
then crawl back again ; we snarl at and undermine each other ; we play, with
unbecoming zeal, " much ado about nothing " for a few years : we die some day,
just when we did not want to ; the living clod is resolved into the lifeless one, and
we become a dream—a recollection—a dimly remembered thing, of whom, perchance, some singular custom or odd saying is recorded, at intervals, for a brief
space of time, and then (to all worldly intents and purposes) we are as if we
had never been.

But to return to Edmonstone, who began to retrace some part of his way, in
order to command a better view of the road the stage travelled. In descending, he encountered the scent—fragrant in the open air—of burning wood, and
was presently stopped by a forest nymph, with a cloak, carelesly flung on her shoulders,
emerging from the coppice. She threw herself in his path, probably with a view
of preventing approach to the encampment, which could not be far off, and which
he had no wish to pry into, for the gipsies enjoyed a dubious reputation, and the
males of the tribe were thought rather dangerous when encountered by a lone
traveller.

She will know the country around, he thought, and might possibly lead him to
the very place where the object of his romantic attachment was imprisoned. He
regretted that Francis was not present, for the valet confessedly knew more of the
earl's movements than he divulged, although in other respects as zealous as his
master in the search. They knew that Constance was carried to some house in
that country, but the earl, so far as they could learn, possessed neither property
nor connexions there.

The girl's eyes sparkled on beholding a half-guinea—silver was the ordinary
fee.

" What will you promise me for this ?" asked the merchant.

The hand was carefully perused, though her eyes were oft turned to
examine his dress, features, and whatever might aid the magic of the art.

" I read good fortune and the speedy accomplishment of your wishes," replied
the sybil, gazing on his face.

" I hope it will be speedy—I am indeed tired of travelling—I have been
several days on horseback, and would give you as much gold as would cover both
those nut-brown hands, if you could guide me to where I am bound."

" Gold—more gold," cried the girl with surprise, " it rains gold—where do you
come from, stranger ?"

" Ah ! is your craft at fault ?" exclaimed Arthur, laughing ; " if you know
not whence I came, surely you cannot tell whither I am bound.'

The girl blushed. Taking his fingers, she balanced the hand, that the sun's
light might more clearly show the tracery of the minute lines which are supposed
to indicate the clashing interests of life. But on hearing the sound of carriage-
wheels, he turned away abruptly ; the stage passed into the village ; it stopped
above a minute ; was again in motion, and he beheld, to his exceeding satisfaction, the coach which contained the exacting spinster, driven beyond the precincts
of the hamlet.

The sudden disregard of the sybil's predictions, and the abruptness with which
he withdrew his hand, awoke her ire, and she turned to depart.

" Stay, stay !" cried Arthur.

She heeded not the summons ; but he had no intention she should depart
without submitting to the questions he was about to propose. He caught hold of
her cloak—she released it from her throat, and confronted with flashing eye, the
importunate applicant.

The removal of the cloak dislodged a card from her apparel—it fell on the ground. Arthur stooped, and picked it up.

"The seven of hearts," said Edmonstone, smiling, "seven is, I have heard, a mysterious number."

The girl endeavoured to snatch it from him, but did not succeed. By chance, the back turned upward; and to his exceeding surprise, he beheld in slight, black characters, the name of Bennington, and the number of the good lady's house in Tavistock-street.

Arthur turned pale. Did these gipsies really deal in the black art? What mystery was here! The words were evidently scratched by the writer with a sharp, or pointed instrument; charcoal dust rubbed over the inscription made it distinct and legible. That the card was in some way connected with the fate of Constance he could not doubt.

Thank heaven for this discovery! How fortunate the rencontre with the impracticable Miss Priscilla Woodberry—how foolishly and blindly does man judge of events! He had been internally cursing the cruel destiny which threw him in the way of the importunate spinster; yet she was the cause (though indirect) of his present delight.

"Who gave you this card?" asked Arthur, with deep anxiety.

"No one; I took it from the pack," replied the girl " 'tis a lucky number, but I fear my luck changed when the card fell."

"Have done with this foolery," cried Arthur, with impatience, "here is gold—guineas as many as you can count—complain not of change of luck, but tell me quickly where you obtained this card. These words, I suspect, were written by a lady, young, beautiful, and in affliction—was it not so? And the Benningtons, have you seen them—sent to them? Keep me not in suspense. I am a friend of the lady who gave you this token, and am now in search of her."

The surprise of the fortune-teller, whilst listening to this discourse, equalled that of the speaker. Throwing aside her reserve, she narrated all that she knew respecting Constance. Two hours since she had conversed with her at the window of her chamber, till—as we have already narrated—their conference was cut short. Arthur was highly alarmed at the peril which threatened Constance—he feared that she would be removed on board ship before he could hinder it. He could not account for the tardiness of Le Raincy's friends. The messenger had been fully instructed what to say to the Benningtons—and lest he should blunder, carried a letter from one of the tribe, who had learned to write.

The position of Constance was so critical, that Arthur decided on making an attempt at rescue without waiting for aid from London. But before he resolved his plans, Francis was summoned to council, and made acquainted with the unexpected discovery.

Henderson's abode was about six miles distant; the route was unfrequented, but the road was practicable for carriages. It was agreed, that the fortune-teller's kindred should be consulted and their assistance evoked. The girl, who had waited at the hillock the return of Mr. Edmonstone with his servant, led the way to the encampment—a ruined barn. The gipsy girl was in high glee at the prospect of beating up the quarters of Captain Henderson, who had, according to her report, caused two of her brothers to be transported to the plantations in Virginia for some offence, which though punishable by law, was deemed no infraction of the code of gipsy morality. On arrival, the men—some half dozen sturdy fellows—readily agreed to assist Mr. Edmonstone, and were much pleased with the liberal payment offered. In addition to other grievances, Arthur learned they were excessively chagrined at being obliged to quit the old manor-house, which they had begun to regard in the light of a lawful inheritance, and which they found very convenient whilst carrying on a smuggling trade with the masters of certain sailing-craft which crossed the channel. It was true, no direct confession was made of these practices, but half a word to the young merchant sufficed to reveal the nature of their operations. One important fact was, however, very evident; Arthur need entertain no fear of treachery from his allies. They had a strong hatred toward Henderson, and an equally strong motive for wishing the lady restored to her friends. The disappearance of the suite of servants, who came, as it were, by magic, would follow the removal of the prisoner, and the house, without doubt, be abandoned to its former tenants.

It was next discussed, whether they should attempt an assault, or resort to stratagem. The gipsies advised the latter. They had their private reasons, doubtless, for preferring stratagem. It was no part of their policy to shed blood, (which must ensue in a contest,) and which of course would bring on them the eye of the law, when in truth they courted obscurity and secresy. But it was not difficult to urge very plausible reasons for eschewing force, unless in case of necessity. Henderson's garrison nearly doubled their numbers, including Mr. Edmonstone and Francis. There was, in addition, the crew of the yacht, between which and the house—as the gipsies observed—a constant communication was kept up, and signals continually exchanged. 'Twere madness, therefore, to incur certain defeat, when their object might be attained by skill and secresy. They had already established a communication with the prisoner—why not use the same mode to effect her escape? If they were discovered, it would be time enough to make a show of hostility to cover the retreat of the lady.

These arguments prevailed. Money was furnished by Edmonstone to engage a post-chaise and four horses, with relays for several stages in advance. It could hardly be expected that the lady would be borne off without creating an alarm ; but if they only suceeded in placing her in the chaise, however closely they might be pressed, and however superior in numbers the captain's force, her escape was beyond doubt.

Such was the plan of attack. To each man was assigned his post of occupation —to the gipsy-girl was allotted the task of awaiting in the chaise, the arrival of Constance, in order that the lady might not travel without the presence of one of her own sex. Edmonstone had a more important part to perform than keeping company with Le Raincy in her flight. It was essential that he staid to cover her retreat, and in the event of conflict, to give sanction, by his presence, to the action of the gipsies, who might otherwise incur the odium and penalty of committing a daring violation of peace and order, without a motive, or legal extenuation.

Meanwhile the sun was declining, and the hour approached for the commencement of the exploit.

CHAPTER XX.

CONSTANCE sat alone, in fearful expectation either of the announcement of a fatal issue of the wound she had inflicted, or, on the other hand—an alternative yet more calamitous—that if the earl found himself out of danger, the threat of carrying her to the ship would be executed.

With locked door, she listened attentively to catch some sound, or some sign, which might indicate the state of his lordship. There was a hurrying to and fro, but no one came near her apartment—it seemed as though she was forgotten.

The dusk of the evening grew apace, but no one, as usual, brought lights. She threw herself in the chair, and sat brooding over her bitter fate. Suddenly she saw something moving outside the window—it was an apparition which she had learned to welcome. On looking steadily, she discerned a man's hand, waving between his fingers, a letter. 'Twas a friendly signal, and her heart leaped with joy. She flew to the window, and opening it gently, reached out her hand for the letter, but he withdrew it. Surprised at the action, she inquired if the letter were intended for her why he should refuse to surrender it.

"Hush! hush!" replied he, "the letter is nothing. I feared if you saw my face you would create an alarm. Thank Heaven, we are all right so far, but these bars are tough—could you not creep between!"'

"Alas! no! or I would have flung myself from the window before now. Do you come from my friends—from London?"

The man then spoke a few words to some one below. Presently the speaker's head was lifted, and, after examining the bars, he whispered that there was no help but to saw through the wood, and risk the noise. Their force, he said, was much inferior to the garrison, or they would have approached in a different fashion, and it was feared, if an alarm were raised, that she might be removed before aid could be summoned from town.

The fellow was not idle, but, even while he spoke, applied a small saw to the oaken bar. He did not dare move it rapidly, yet the wood was hard, and but little progress made. Each stroke vibrated keenly on the nerves of Constance. The man told her to go to the room-door and listen—if she heard a footstep to give him a signal, and he would cease.

The earl's disaster disarranged the ordinary economy of the establishment. The housekeeper was doubtless in attendance on her master; she had never before been such a while absent. The noise of the saw at length ceased, and Constance, flying to the window, was informed that the bar was severed.

"Is Mr. Bennington there?" asked the half-frantic prisoner.

"No! no! ask no questions—our work is not done yet."

A knotted rope was affixed to the bar above the one severed. Soon as this operation was complete, Constance was told that on removal of the other bar, there would be space wide enough for her to pass through; but that the noise of wrenching it away would probably raise an alarm. He bade her stand aside whilst his companion, mounting by the rope, gained the window-sill, and, both applying their strength, succeeded in bursting the fractured bar inward, with a crash and rebound which justified the warning.

"Now! now!" cried the men.

Constance was hastily dragged through, and the trio rapidly descended. As soon as they reached the ground, she was led through the shrubbery, and lifted over the paling into a meadow or paddock. The spokesman desired her to run quickly, for were she overtaken her friends would be outnumbered, and she would be carried back. But in quickness of flight, our heroine needed no prompting. The agility acquired in the exercise of her profession enabled her, with ease, to outstrip both. On reaching the opposite fence, she was lifted into the road by a gentleman, who addressed her by name, said he was a friend of the Benningtons, and expressed his happiness on beholding her freed from detention. Yonder chaise, he said, was in waiting, and she would travel under the escort of Francis, his valet and the gipsey-girl, whom she knew, and on whose fidelity she might rely. These words were spoken whilst hastening to the vehicle. Constance inquired why he staid behind; and expressed a wish to remain under the protection of a friend of Mr. Bennington, rather than proceed under the uncertain escort of a domestic and her gipsey ally.

"I would gladly accompany you," said the gentleman, very hurriedly, as he handed her into the chaise, "yet there are not many of us, and yonder house contains more than a dozen—besides, there is a cutter riding at anchor, and I have reason to believe, if you were once more wrested from us, we should not know where to seek you; but I see lights moving; boy, drive on—Francis, to your place—farewell, Constance, till we meet again in Tavistock-street."

The chaise rattled on, but the words, "farewell Constance," from a stranger, long dwelt in her ear; her fingers long retained his parting pressure. Who was he? Good heavens, could it be Arthur Edmonstone? The thought was startling, yet was too pleasing to be dismissed.—But we must leave these interesting speculations, which found a place in her breast, even midst the tumult of feelings consequent on the extraordinary events of the evening, so far happily crowned by an unexpected escape from the worst of perils, to return to Arthur and his party,

It was certain that Constance was missed, and a pursuit commencing. Mr. Edmonstone summoned his people from the spot where they stood in ambush, and gave instructions. In a few minutes, two horsemen and several followers on foot, came along at a quick space. Arthur's force took possession of the centre of the road, and challenged the advancing party. The horsemen made light of the challenge, and were about to ride through the obstruction, when a threat to use fire-arms if they did not immediately halt, had the intended effect. The leader, with

THE GYPSEY AT THE WINDOW COMMUNICATES WITH CONSTANCE.

much indignation, demanded the cause of being stopped on the king's highway, and threatened his audacious adversaries with the rigour of the law.

Arthur replied that the penalty of the law would fall on those who had broken it; that of late, this part of the country was infested by suspicious characters; that a daring outrage had been perpetrated, and he would not allow them to continue their journey till they returned to the first house on the road, that he might have an opportunity of seeing their faces, and learning something satisfac-tory about their intentions. The horseman swore many a round oath, and called

No. 11.

to his servants to knock down the insolent marauders, but they were as loath as the doughty captain himself to advance on the long, threatening pistols held out *in terrorem* in their faces.

Arthur's object was, of course, to gain time, in which he was not unsuccessful. Whilst wrangling, there came to the encounter, hobbling and running, an elderly man, in a loose dressing-gown, without hat or wig.

"Where is she?" he cried, "have you not caught this mad wench?"

"Back, back, sir," exclaimed the captain, "consider your state of health, and loss of blood—Sirrah! lead back your master."

"Ah! my Lord Headington," shouted Arthur, "if I did not fear your lordship would catch cold from the night-air, I would ask you who is this mounted gentleman, who talks so loudly? Will your lordship declare his name and vouch for his honesty, that I may let him pass?"

"And who are you, I would ask, who pretend to address me by a name I have no title to?"

"Ah! my lord," replied the other, "it is vain to attempt concealing your rank; the air and spirit of the gentleman breaks through every disguise. I am here, my lord in search of an evil-doer, who has committed a foul wrong. I do suspect this man on horseback; if he is a friend of your lordship, pray inform me of his name and station, that I may make amends for the detention."

The captain threw out a volley of oaths, and turning his horse's head, ordered his people home. If it were not for the fire-arms, he would, he said, ride over these insolent ruffians; but to-morrow they should suffer what they merited." With much ado Henderson succeeded in dragging home the earl, who raved after the mad wench.

Both Edmonstone and the other party, were now convinced that the fugitive was beyond the reach of the latter. Arthur said he should be found at the inn, in the village, till the hour of ten to-morrow morning, and so ended the skirmish, fortunately without bloodshed.

About nine o'clock, just as he had concluded breakfast, the card of Capt Henderson was handed by the waiter. Before receiving his visitor, Arthur made inquiry, and learned that he was a ruined spendthrift, who once owned a marine villa in the neighbourhood, and still occupied it by sufferance, though the property was in the power of his creditors. The earl it appeared from the waiter's report, was unknown in that part of the country, and his arrival at the lone villa, a secret which had not yet transpired. These particulars confirmed what Arthur already knew, and he desired the captain to be introduced.

After asking Edmonstone his name and place of residence, Henderson said, that through what had passed last night, there was but one alternative, and inquired if he had a friend at hand.

"You act, I suppose, for Lord Headington?"

Henderson affected surprise at the question—wondered what privilege Mr. Edmonstone had to make use of the name of a nobleman to whom he was a stranger, and who, by the last news from town, was now with the court. It was himself to whom the insult was offered, and he desired to know the name of Mr. Edmonstone's friend, that proper arrangements for a meeting might be made without delay.

Arthur replied that the persons of both the Earl of Headington and Captain Henderson were too well known to him to make a mistake in their identity. He had seen them often together at the opera-house, and knew the vile purpose for which they met. He was proud to say that he was successful in rescuing Mademoiselle Le Raincy from their toils. He had already written to London for a friend to join him. If his lordship claimed reparation, he would afford the satisfaction required, but he had no intention to allow the earl to fight by proxy. If it suited his lordship's plans to employ panderers to aid him in his unworthy pursuits, let them keep their proper obscurity when questions of honour were discussed. He would, he said, wait till noon, to-morrow, for a communication from his lordship, and meantime a friend would be on the way from London,

Henderson, scarcely holding his smothered resentment under controul, threatened if Mr. Edmonstone refused the meeting, to inflict personal chastisement on him. Arthur said, if he attempted it he would treat him as he would a highway-man.

The captain then softened, and said he was persuaded Mr. Edmonstone, after mature consideration, would behave with more courtesy to one who was by birth and education, a gentleman. Arthur observed in reply that he had undertaken, in connection with the friends of Mlle. Le Raincy, to rescue her from the power of Lord Headington. He had accomplished his purpose, and if any one were aggrieved, it was the earl, not an agent of the earl. If his lordship declined the quarrel, it was not for one who acted as his tool to take it up—still he had no desire, unnecessarily, to cast any indignity on one whom he presumed bore his majesty's commission; and, after affording the earl the satisfaction of a meeting, he would afterward, if able, extend the same courtesy to Captain Henderson. But in no case would he meet the captain if the earl declined—his lordship must, and should fight his own battles. He would wait at the inn till the time before mentioned. Henderson departed much dissatisfied—baulked of his chance of marrying Le Raincy, and by the course assumed by Edmonstone, baulked also of the revenge which he desired to gratify in hostile conflict with the man who had spoiled his finely-planned schemes.

Twelve o'clock next day, arrived, and two o'clock, and yet no message from the villa. It was obvious my lord backed out. Arthur next gave a farewell audience to his body-guard. They were paid above their expectations, Arthur promising, moreover, to keep their secrets, which chance had revealed. He offered to place the young gipsy-girl in a different and more comfortable sphere of life than the one which she now followed. But the proposal was peremptorily, though respectfully, declined. They never forsook their habits, and certainly Letty would not depart from the customs of her ancestors. Finding entreaty and persuasion alike useless, Mr. Edmonstone promised to send back Letty to Hampshire, on his return to London, if she had not already found her way thither.

He then ordered horses, leaving with the landlord his address in Austin-Friars, lest it should be called for. On the way, he kept a sharp look out for Neville, whom he trusted to intercept. About forty miles from London a letter was put into his hands, with the signature of Mr. Bennington, with the news, that the latter, properly accompanied, was on his route to Hampshire, when to his joy and surprise, he fell in with Constance, whom he accompanied home, as there was no longer occasion for himself or his posse to continue the journey.

Neville met his friend about twenty miles from London, and they returned to town together. He fully approved of the position Arthur had taken—the system of introducing gladiators into society to fight cowards' battles merited contempt and execration. Neville, as usual, was much disposed to rally his friend, but the latter prayed relief till they met again.

And how was Arthur received in Tavistock-street? With much chiding, mingled with tears—reproof that he should have so long abstained visiting his playmate, and suffered her to entertain harsh thoughts of the friend of her child-hood. Yet the meeting was deeply fraught with happiness, and revived the happiness of their earlier years. It was with delight that Constance found that her visit to Kensington was known to Arthur—though appearances were otherwise, he had not forgotten the old spot, nor had he forsaken it. Another visit, in company with Mrs. Bennington and Arthur, several days after his arrival, was to Constance the sweetest day of her life.

By some means, the enterprise of the Earl of Headington, and his discomfiture got wind, and on the occasion of his visiting the court, after the breaking up of parliament, and the season of fashions, the monarch turned his back on the peer, a hint which was not lost on his lordship. He quitted England for a tour on the continent of Europe, which was prolonged into a residence abroad of some years' duration.

Letty the gipsy-girl, was dismissed with many presents. She justified the prediction of her kindred, though perhaps fears of their ill-will might exert a secret influence in causing her to refuse the liberal offers of Mr. Edmonstone. Arthur took a pleasure in narrating his adventure with the stage-coach passengers. To Miss Priscilla Woodberry he owed a lasting debt of gratitude—perhaps the future happiness of Constance and himself was owing to the ungallant aversion of the young man, which led him to the discovery of Le Raincy's place of durance. A day later she would have been carried off to sea. To Arthur, however, was never afforded the opportunity of uttering his thanks to the fair spinster.

Francis earned the promised reward from his master, of five hundred guineas, but he did not quit his service. And as Mr. Edmonstone admitted, he well deserved the recompense, for without his aid, it might have proved impossible to discover the direction taken by those who carried off Mlle. Le Raincy, so adroitly and secretly was the abduction planned.

The manager tried, but ineffectually, to engage the danseuse for another season. She preferred yielding to Arthur's solicitations, and became his bride before the summer was over. Need we add, that a union, originating in the intimacy and friendship of childhood, cherished in memory through youth, and renewed at maturity, was happy? The royal patroness of our heroine was pleased that she had found a protector who would remove her from a station so exposed to peril, to the comfort and security of private life—though her majesty could not help regretting the loss of talents whose exhibition had afforded her so much delight.

We have only to add, that the Benningtons continued to prosper till the good lady retired from Tavistock-street, to enjoy, in dignity and ease, the ample fortune she had earned and saved, and that Captain Henderson never recovered from merited poverty and neglect.

THE END.